WHEN JUSTICE HAS CLAWS

WHEN JUSTICE HAS CLAWS
DRAKETHORN LEGAL™
BOOK SIX

ISABEL CAMPBELL
MICHAEL ANDERLE

This book is a work of fiction. All of the characters, organizations, and events portrayed in this novel are either products of the author's imagination or are used fictitiously. Sometimes both.

Copyright © 2024 LMBPN Publishing
Cover by Mihaela Voicu http://www.mihaelavoicu.com/
Cover copyright © LMBPN Publishing
A Michael Anderle Production

LMBPN Publishing supports the right to free expression and the value of copyright. The purpose of copyright is to encourage writers and artists to produce the creative works that enrich our culture.

The distribution of this book without permission is a theft of the author's intellectual property. If you would like permission to use material from the book (other than for review purposes), please contact support@lmbpn.com. Thank you for your support of the author's rights.

LMBPN® Publishing
2375 E. Tropicana Avenue, Suite 8-305
Las Vegas, Nevada 89119 USA

Version 1.00, November 2024
ebook ISBN: 979-8-89354-274-5
Print ISBN: 979-8-89354-275-2

THE WHEN JUSTICE HAS CLAWS TEAM

Thanks to the JIT Readers

Christopher Gilliard
Veronica Stephan-Miller
Diane L. Smith
Jeff Goode
Sean Kesterson
Zacc Pelter
Dorothy Lloyd
Peter Manis
Jan Hunnicutt
Daryl McDaniel

If I've missed anyone, please let me know!

Editor
The SkyFyre Editing Team

CHAPTER ONE

The salty air blew off the Atlantic ocean, scattering Amy's slightly damp, blonde hair across her face. The wind was cold and piercing, and she clutched her raincoat around her body. *Not long now.* She was almost there. Almost had everything she needed.

Distant thunder rumbled. Lightning streaked across the dark sky. She hoped it wouldn't rain until she had finished the job.

Amy pushed her hair out of her eyes and peered at the people ahead. In the dim twilight, she had to stay close to see where the men were going. Only the full moon occasionally moving out from behind strings of heavy clouds and the lights on nearby docks and the buildings lining the small town past the beach gave her light.

The shadows concealed her from the men she was pursuing. If they sensed that she was following, they didn't show it. Amy wished for a moment that she could become one with her surroundings like Kiera. She wasn't paranormal, however. She had to remind herself that this wasn't a disadvantage. Stacy had sent *her*, not Kiera, for a reason.

The small town on the coast of Maine was known for its pristine Victorian summer houses and the wealthy folk who frequented them. The houses were not rented out, so they were empty much of the time. Winter was coming. Mid-November in this part of Maine was a beautiful time for Amy to walk the streets in a heavy jacket, admiring the last of the autumn foliage. She was not there to admire her surroundings, though.

No one should have been in town until Christmas, when the buildings lining the main street were adorned with wreaths and twinkling white lights and the pavement was dusted with snow.

Why were these men here?

Skipping town, Amy thought. In New York City, the denizens of the underworld were being rooted out one crook at a time. These men were among the many who'd dealt in illicit drugs, and though they were human, they were connected to the paranormals that infested the underworld like cockroaches. While Kiera dispatched the paranormals in the city, Amy went to places like this to deal with the others.

The men were heading for a dock and a boat. Where they planned to go, she did not care as long as they were leaving. She had the evidence.

The boat rocked in the churning waves. A light on board illuminated the dock, soon to be slick with rain. The storm had arrived, and Amy did not envy these men their journey. They had to leave, though. Who knew what wrath Stacy Drakethorn would send after them?

Amy was close enough to snap photos, and the light on the boat helped her camera distinguish their faces without using the flash. Several photos later, her task was complete. She began mentally writing her exposé.

Vincent Jones and Alessandro Giovanni skip town after twenty-six-year-old attorney-heiress Stacy Drakethorn exposes them for trafficking drugs using a property owned by one of her clients. Jones and Giovanni were influential members of New York City's elite society, but few were aware of their underworld activities until now. Longtime associates of the late Victor Corbinelli, the men were well-connected and privileged.

They held influence and financial power in New York City through their business and real estate ventures. This article will discuss their lives, their careers, and their downfall.

Ideas flowed through Amy's mind, bringing a faint smile to her lips. The boat departed. Let them run. The FBI would deal with them. She would let everyone know that her friend Stacy was dismantling the festering darkness beneath their beloved city.

Amy headed back up the beach toward the town and the tiny inn she'd stayed in during her investigation. Lightning struck close by, and thunder cracked. Rain pelted her as she passed the rocks that flanked a narrow, sandy path that led to the parking lot at the back of a seafood restaurant. Past the restaurant and down a block was the inn. Amy reached it and stepped inside, breathing a sigh of relief.

Thunder shook the building. The windows rattled, but the warmth of the Tiffany lamps and the fire crackling in the salon welcomed her. Amy was the only guest.

"You poor dear!" the elderly woman behind the welcome desk exclaimed when she entered. "You shouldn't have gone out."

Amy produced a smile. "After I've showered and warmed up, I'll be fine, Mrs. Peterson. Thank you."

"I'll have some tea brought up to your room. Have you had dinner?"

Amy shook her head, although her rumbling stomach told the woman that she hadn't eaten since breakfast.

Mrs. Peterson smiled warmly. "I'll bring that up too."

Amy was glad that the woman didn't press for more details. She would have loved to stay another day. The residents of this town were among the most pleasant she'd ever met. "Thank you, Mrs. Peterson. I'd love that."

From a perch on the desk, a black cat named Princess fixed large green eyes on Amy. She was ninety percent sure the cat was male but had been mistakenly identified as female and named accordingly. The dubious expression the cat gave her seemed to say, *"What* were *you doing out there in the rain?"*

Amy grinned as she headed to her room on the second floor. The cat hopped down from the desk and trailed her as she had trailed those men throughout the day. She whispered, "I wonder what you're like when you're not in cat form."

Upstairs, Amy selected dry clothes from her suitcase and headed for the bathroom. She hadn't bothered unpacking, only expecting to be here a couple of days. "Tomorrow, I will go home," she murmured. Amy glanced over her shoulder at the cat who had hopped onto her bed and grinned. "Sorry we didn't have more time to get acquainted, Princess."

Damien Hartwell wanted to be in bed, but he was still waiting. The grandfather clock in the corner of his study seemed to be ticking louder than normal tonight, or perhaps it was the silence in the house that drew his attention to the irritating *tick-tock, tick-tock.*

He sat in a leather armchair by the window, his dark eyes sweeping the shadows that had gathered on the vacant grounds in anticipation of the dawn, which was still hours away. Aside from the solitary candle flickering on the desk, the room was dark. That did not matter. When his guest arrived, he would feel the person's power. Damien didn't need to see.

He sighed, checking the clock again. Only a minute had passed. It was nearing two. Damien's eyes strayed to the paper on his desk, his handwriting scrawled across it in black ink. The letter was not yet finished. He'd been reworking it for days. When he sent it, he hoped she would say yes.

She would be foolish not to, he thought.

Stacy Drakethorn had dealt with foes such as Victoria Corbinelli and Gregory Hines, both of whom Damien, who worked for the FBI, had thoroughly researched. Though he'd not been involved in either investigation, their demises traced to one person: an attorney from New York City who'd formerly gone by the shortened version of her name, Stacy Drake. Apparently, inheriting her father's resources had caused her to resume her full name.

Damien smirked. He and Stacy had much in common. He thought about his mother and what he knew about Stacy's.

Though Damien had found much on Corbinelli and Hines, researching Stacy Drakethorn had been more challenging. He'd learned where she had gone to college and worked afterward. Her current location and employment status were still unknown. She also hadn't appeared in court for months. Strange, given her reputation and desire to help the less fortunate. What the hell was she doing?

Damien went to the desk, dropped into the swivel chair behind it, and surveyed what he'd written so far. He could send an email or call her, but this seemed the better route given the contents of the letter. He wouldn't want it falling into the wrong hands.

Damien picked up the pen, noticing that the candle was burning low. He'd hardly pressed the pen to the paper when a chill darted up his spine, raising the hairs on the back of his neck. His guest was here.

Damien set the pen down and straightened, not wanting to show fear. Not that it mattered. His guest would sense it. "Hello?" Damien croaked.

He heard a swish as if a cloak had brushed the floorboards. No footsteps, though. No feet weighing down the boards in this old house enough to make them creak.

The man appeared at last.

Damien wasn't certain if he had been here the entire time, masked by the shadows, or if he had materialized out of thin air. Regardless, his appearance unnerved Damien.

The tall man had an ancient, regal voice. "Hello, Hartwell." He pushed back a dark hood, revealing long, silver hair tucked behind his pointed ears.

Damien swallowed. He'd never seen a fae before, though he had imagined what they would be like for a long time. "It's late."

"I had other matters to attend to," the fae stated. He gestured at the unfinished letter. "You should have finished writing that by now."

Damien agreed, but he had to restrain himself from retorting, "I had other matters to attend to."

The fae sighed. "I thought you humans had better methods of communication." He surveyed the dim room, sniffing. Damien had not bothered to change anything in the study since his father's death ten years ago. The oak walls and mahogany desk did not seem to be up to this fae's standards, but Damien didn't care. He had preserved his father's legacy and the Hartwell home.

Damien's remaining family lived on the other side of the country and wanted nothing to do with him. They'd considered his father cruel and prejudiced. Damien had thought his father reasonable. He didn't mind living in the mansion alone. He had staff, and though it could be lonely, he preferred to work without others hovering over him.

The fae's eyes strayed to a portrait of Damien's father that hung above the mantle. Damien wondered if the fae was thinking that his father and Damien looked similar. He had his father's dark hair, brown eyes, proud brow, and lips and was as attractive as his father had been when he was thirty-five.

Damien's personality mirrored his mother's. Damien's father had been outspoken, brash, and ambitious. His mother had been reserved, cunning, and clever. She'd planned everything meticulously, which had eventually allowed her to escape her cruel husband. *And leave me behind,* Damien thought bitterly.

The fae did not need to know that. He also did not need to know that Damien's mother had been a witch.

"I don't see why you're bothering," the fae drawled. "The Drakethorn heir will say no. You have little idea how stubborn dragons can be."

Damien was aware of the many paranormals that lived among them. Most who worked for the FBI were. Damien knew about witches and shifters like Victor Corbinelli, who was a werewolf. He had studied dragons for years. He still could not quite wrap his mind around having dragons living in their world, much less that Stacy Drakethorn was one. The fae before him had come from another world. Few fae lived on Earth.

The fae drifted closer, scrutinizing Damien as he braced his hands on the desk. The furniture creaked beneath the seemingly ethereal being's weight. "The veil will come down, regardless of what the dragon girl agrees to. You may continue with your plan, Hartwell, but I will see her dead in the end."

Damien hoped that would not be the case. He needed Stacy for his private purposes. *You lured him here,* Damien reminded himself. If the fae created chaos, it was Damien's fault. This could turn into a major fuck-up.

The male reached into his cloak and pulled out a thin scroll. It bounced when he tossed it on Damien's desk. "That is all you need to know, Hartwell." The fae vanished as quickly and seamlessly as he had appeared. Damien shivered as he reached for the scroll and removed the string that bound it.

Thorn Estate

The address was scrawled beneath those words. Stacy Drakethorn's location, at last. He would send the letter by messenger tomorrow.

Damien rolled the scroll back up and reached for the pen once more. Before he could set it to paper, however, the candle went out.

CHAPTER TWO

"This is the most important decision of the day, hands down," Stacy Drakethorn told her boyfriend Ethan as she slid into a chair by the kitchen table. "What are we going to do about dinner?"

It was 8:00 p.m., but both had been so busy that this was the first time they could consider their stomachs. The warm kitchen glowed as the chilly night air pressed against the windows. Many of the estate's sprites had come inside and were enjoying the fire from a distance.

Ethan glanced at her from where he stood by the counter, sorting the pile of mail they had received today, a small smile tugging at his lips. "Too bad Rowan sent Kiera on another errand. One of these days, I hope the errand she goes on is a grocery run."

Stacy grabbed her phone. "Take out it is! Thai tonight?"

Ethan nodded. "You know what I want."

Rowan sending Kiera on an errand was code for taking an enemy out. She generally left shortly after sunset to stalk the city and returned before dawn to make breakfast, manage their growing staff's assignments for the day, and then go to bed. In the past several weeks, Stacy had seen little of the estate's housekeeper. She made a mental note to remind Rowan to give Kiera a break. With Amy out of town, Stacy was outnumbered by males.

We need to up the estrogen level here, she thought.

"Even Rowan can't complain about takeout when we order Thai food," Stacy replied as she searched the number for the nearest Thai place.

"Miles went into town for supplies," Ethan reminded her. "You can ask him to pick it up."

Stacy shot a text to the estate's groundskeeper with the request, along with their orders and a reminder that Miles could use the estate's credit card to pay for it. Her stomach rumbled. She'd had breakfast and lunch, but the meals had been hurried affairs. Given her dragon nature, no meal felt like enough. Stacy felt like a pre-teen hitting a growth spurt. Though she was no longer growing, Stacy had to transform into a dragon and fly across her father's estate at least once a week. She thrived under pressure, but these days, she felt like she could not keep her head above water.

Ethan set the mail aside. Nothing important. He leaned against the counter, folding his arms. "When does Amy get back?"

"Tomorrow, I think. She called earlier to tell me she got everything she needed but didn't give me the deets. She'll tell us when she gets back."

"You think Jones and whoever the other guy was got away?"

Stacy shrugged. "Doesn't matter since I only asked Amy to get the story. The FBI can take care of the rest."

Ethan chuckled as he strode over to her and bent to place a kiss on her forehead. "I love it when you let the country's law enforcement officers take care of things, but it's really hot when you do it yourself."

"Literally hot, thanks to me being a fire-breathing dragon."

Ethan chuckled again and sat on the other chair. "Well, with

Jones and the other drug dealers now out of the way, you can focus on other things."

"Like?" Stacy prodded. She'd been swamped since she'd dealt with Cassius, Lenora, and Valen, who were vampires. She was dismantling the underworld one criminal at a time through various means. She bought some people's property out from under them, took others to court, and sent Kiera after the rest. The list had been long but was getting shorter every day.

"We have a meeting in the morning with a young witch who is interested in joining our coven," Ethan reminded her.

"Clara, right?"

Ethan nodded. "Clara Stoneward. She's the daughter of a longtime acquaintance of Rowan's. He's never met her but says her father is trustworthy."

"That's enough for me," Stacy chirped. "We can feel her out tomorrow." Their coven currently had five practitioners. Stacy wasn't in any rush. She would add members as the right people came along. They had to be dedicated and trustworthy but also humble, teachable, and willing to spend a lot of time at her country home.

Since becoming more involved in the paranormal community, Stacy had met other young witches who wanted to join her coven. However, Stacy had discovered that most simply wanted to take advantage of her position and influence.

Ethan was managing the coven. She focused on removing the gangs and cartels, which was much like breaking up the squabbles of petulant children. In her spare time, she was training witches. It was the life balance she'd sought for years.

I'll be glad when I no longer have Victor's cockroaches to deal with, she thought. Six weeks ago, she had prevented a group of vampires from enacting a ritual that would bring an ancient warlock back from the dead. They'd lost Luna, a werewolf she'd intended to bring into their coven, in the fight. Not a day had gone by since then when Stacy didn't have to surmount the grief and guilt she felt over losing the young wolf. She nudged the feeling away.

Ethan was talking to Miles on the phone, frowning at his questions. "That's right. No, Stacy sent you our orders. Well, read the text again!" Miles yammered on before hanging up. Ethan shook his head, sighing.

"He's had a long day too." Stacy reached for Ethan's hand. They all had long days. Rowan and Miles were running the Thorn estate without Stacy's help since she had the underworld matters on her plate, plus dealing with her father's estate.

At one time, Stacy had declined to associate with Constantine Drakethorn. Now he was gone, and she didn't know when he would return. She figured Khan wanted her to be responsible for his estate in the US but stay off-balance since she didn't know when he would come back to check on her and it.

After the vampire ordeal six weeks ago, Khan had told Stacy that he was leaving to have a stern discussion with the vampire factions in Europe. Stacy had thought it wouldn't take long, but it turned out that Khan intended to remain for a time, "So no one gets any ideas about coming over to our side of the pond."

Stacy had been grateful that she wouldn't have to deal with those extremist blood-suckers. She had not, however, expected that he'd hand over his United States possessions to her when he left.

The country estate that bordered hers in upstate New York would have been plenty, but he had several others. She would have to visit and determine if they were worth keeping. They might be better off as public land, or maybe she'd bequeath the properties to werewolf packs who needed the space to run and hunt. Stacy had ideas but had not yet had the time to visit the properties and make the determination.

One step at a time.

It surprised Stacy to learn from the butler that Khan's holdings in Europe were greater still. "He has at least a dozen castles,"

Reginald had explained. "Old musty places. He's never had them cleaned out. Not that anyone would do that as well as I could, mind you."

Stacy smiled at the memory. She didn't know where she would be without Regi and Esme and Torin, the estate's butler, housekeeper, and groundskeeper, respectively. Although she was nominally in charge, Reginald, Esme, and Torin ran the estate. Rowan, Miles, and Kiera ran everything else. Her father's trust bolstered her confidence, but she missed him. It hadn't been the same since he'd left.

Seemingly reading Stacy's thoughts, Ethan asked, "Have you heard from him?"

She shrugged. "He sends a letter once in a while. You didn't see one in the mail, did you?"

Ethan shook his head.

Stacy leaned back in the chair. "Each letter is from a different country. Do you know what he told me before he left? 'I was there before the countries were. Of course I have vast holdings in Europe.'" Ethan laughed at Stacy's impression of her father, which included deepening her voice, puffing out her chest, and drawing her eyebrows together. "'I might need to get rid of a few since those vampires decided they could control them in my absence. It's only dinner conversation, though.'"

Ethan raised a brow. "Did he mean that they would be having a conversation at dinner or that the other person would be dinner while he told them what he would do?"

Stacy cringed. "I didn't ask, and I hope he doesn't tell me when he comes back." Khan was centuries old, and it might be a decade or two before he deigned to return. Stacy would live much longer than a human lifespan too, but she didn't want to think about that now.

"Besides coven stuff, what have you been up to today?" she asked Ethan.

For the past six weeks, Ethan had split his time between his shop and her place. When he was at the shop, he researched Malabbra, the dark world they'd learned about as they'd tried to root out the city's vampire threat. They hadn't learned much other than that it was the homeworld of those who wielded dark magic, including vampires and warlocks.

Some said the first dragons came from Malabbra too. Stacy hadn't asked him to, but Ethan had dived headfirst into the research after the vampires were gone. He was merely curious but posited that the information might become useful one day.

"Research has been slow," Ethan admitted. "That's a good thing for now, though. We have enough to do as it is."

The front door opened, and they both peered into the hall. Rowan appeared a moment later, holding a sealed envelope. When Stacy and Ethan deflated in disappointment, he frowned. "What's wrong?"

"We thought you were Miles," was Stacy's glum response.

Rowan put his hands up. "I'm sorry. I'll leave now and come back in my grubby groundskeeper costume. Would that make you happy?"

Ethan grinned. "We were hoping you were Miles with our dinner, but we're happy to see you. What do you have there?"

Rowan turned the envelope over, peering at the wax seal on the back. "This came for you a moment ago, Stacy."

"The mail already came today," Stacy replied.

"This was hand-delivered." Rowan handed her the crisp crème envelope. The wax seal depicted two crossed swords, but she didn't know who it was from. She expected that the signature would tell her. Rowan explained, "A paranormal carrier brought it. I don't know what he was, but he was as wrinkled as a prune."

"Rowan!" Stacy exclaimed. "That's rude."

Rowan shrugged. "He had a scratchy voice, too. Told me it was for 'the missus of the house,' then vanished into thin air."

"Well, he could be anything," Ethan inserted. "Creepy, though. Did he say who it was from?"

Rowan shook his head. "Didn't give me a chance to ask, either."

Stacy studied the handwriting on the front.

Anastasia Drakethorn.

She did not recognize the handwriting but admired its elegance. She turned it over to open it, but the front door opened again. This time, they also heard stomping boots and Miles' loud, cheery voice. "I'm back, kids!"

Ethan smiled. "Dinner's here."

CHAPTER THREE

Kiera Swiftshadow nudged the body with the toe of her boot to check that he was dead. Not that she needed too. Her knife always landed where she intended it to.

She knelt beside the body and rolled him over. The hilt of her favorite dagger caught the glint of the moonlight seeping through the clouds. Kiera tugged it free, and blood poured from the wound. The metallic scent was sharp. He'd been afraid enough to sweat bullets, and the man's face was white, his eyes glassy and unfocused. Kiera closed them with her gloved fingers. She'd killed many in her long life, but she didn't like seeing the emptiness in a person's eyes after the life had left them. She wiped her blade clean on his clothes and sheathed it, intending to give it a proper cleaning when she returned home.

"You were particularly difficult," she told the corpse. "I had to use my best dagger." Its magic not only caused the necessary organs to be pierced but also scorched the man's veins as he died. Kiera stroked the hilt with her gloved hand, thinking about what to do next. She'd waited until the man passed the alley she was in before striking him, and he lay in a narrow space between two brick walls. Kiera pressed close to one, concealed by the shadows. She would not leave the body here. Let whoever came looking for him think he'd run away.

A small smile graced her lips. Perhaps no one would look for him. His employees would be relieved never to see him again. A shifter who could take multiple forms, he often became a large insect. Kiera would have liked to crush him beneath her boot. Cleaning up *that* mess would have been much easier. When she approached, however, he had pissed himself instead of transforming to flee. A damn shame.

Kiera was glad he'd been terrified in his last moments. He'd spent many years frightening others. He'd dealt drugs, forced others to take them, and partaken in gang rapes, murders, and robberies. The city was better off without scum like him.

Kiera wished she had Stacy's list so she could cross this foe off. That was almost as satisfying as taking the life of someone as disgusting as this man had been.

Kiera noticed specks of blood on her gloves and wiped them on her cloak. She had to call someone to haul the body away. She reached back to slip the phone from the back pocket of her pants but tensed instead. Someone had followed her. *Bad night for that, buddy. I'll use my dagger again if I have to.*

Kiera slunk further into the shadows, her enhanced fae and sidhe hearing picking up on light footfalls as someone came toward her. The person wasn't being subtle. Did they intend to get caught?

Kiera waited, breath held, until the person reached the mouth of the alley, then stepped up and held a knife to their throat.

A gangly young man with a white throat gasped and held up his hands. He was slightly taller than Kiera. Freckles dotted his face, and his dark, unkempt hair was stuck to his face and neck. He smelled of cigarette smoke and body odor.

"Why are you following me?" Kiera snarled into his ear, and bumps of terror rose on his bare arms.

"Pl-please," the young man replied. "Let me…" He slowly lowered a hand to the pocket of his jeans and withdrew a small, folded piece of paper. It was crinkled enough for Kiera to know he'd been carrying it for a while.

She snatched it. "What is this?"

"It's for Stacy Dr-drakethorn. You're h-her…um…you work for her, right?" His inquiry was more pleading than curiosity, as if he'd be dead if he gave it to the wrong person.

How the hell did he know she worked for Stacy? Kiera stepped back and lowered her knife, then spun the young man around, pushed him against the brick wall, and grabbed his shirt.

The man's eyes widened. "Y-you're the Dark Angel, aren't you?"

That was an equal amount of awe and fear in his voice. The dark green hood concealed her face. Many within Stacy's and Rowan's paranormal community called her that since they knew Stacy sent her to "take care of business." She was vengeance and reckoning, some said. Kiera didn't care for the moniker, but she'd never expressed that. *I wouldn't mind having wings.*

"How did you find me?" she demanded, letting go of the man's shirt. He was quaking enough not to flee.

"I had help," he admitted. "From wolves."

"I-I'm an elf," he hurried to add, shoving his long hair back to reveal a pointed ear. "Stacy might not remember, but a couple of years ago, she helped my father win a property dispute case. She didn't know we were elves, but she saved us. My family would have lost our ancestral lands and been homeless if not for her. She wasn't a regular lawyer. She actually gave a fuck about us. I w-wanted to thank her by bringing you that." He motioned to the paper.

Kiera frowned as she unfolded it. The paper bore a simple message.

Enemies abound. Someone with great power gathers allies. Be careful, Drakethorn.

What the hell did that mean? "Who gave you this?"

"I-I didn't see him," the man replied. "That is, I didn't see his face. He was…tall." He cringed, seeming to know that wasn't helpful.

Kiera sheathed the knife and folded her arms. The chill wind rustled her cloak.

The young man continued. "He said that if I and 'my people' cared about Stacy Drakethorn, I would get this message to her. I tried to ask who he was, but he disappeared."

"How long ago?"

"Last week. The guy came at me when I was leaving a bar. He wasn't very nice. I knew you'd come around at some point, so I hired three werewolves to track you."

Kiera glanced beyond him.

"They're gone," the young man added.

Figured. The wolves probably sniffed her out, then fled, not wanting to risk her wrath. Kiera wondered if they were from the Graytails pack. Probably not, since they would have come directly to Stacy with the young man and his message. These must be the city wolves who ran fighting pits and bars where they played metal music. There were packs in the city, most brutish and prejudiced against other paranormals. Stacy didn't like to deal with them. The Graytails and their allies were different.

Kiera softened her expression and voice. This guy didn't mean her any harm. "What's your name, kid?"

"David."

"Well, David, you've got balls to come after me like this. I could have fucking killed you."

He nodded vigorously. "I know, but I wanted Stacy to get the message. She's a good person."

A dozen questions flooded her mind. Who'd sent the letter, and what powerful person was rallying Stacy's underworld foes against her? There weren't many left, given Kiera's forays in the night. She held her hand out. "Give me your phone, kid."

David's hand shook as he withdrew his phone and handed it to her. Kiera opened the contacts app and typed Thorn Estate, then the phone number Stacy used for business. "If you hear anything else, call this number. No more following me, okay?"

He nodded.

"Now go home."

David dipped his head, then hurried out of the alley. When he saw the body, he increased his pace.

Kiera chuckled. *That's what you get when you find me after a fresh kill.* When David was gone, Kiera refolded the paper and slipped it into her pocket. She would show it to Stacy when she went home. Right now, she had to deal with the body.

The note repeated her name in the elegant script the envelope bore. Stacy scanned the contents, which were irritatingly vague.

"Well?" Rowan prodded, noting the way Stacy's brows drew together.

Stacy cleared her throat. "I have long wished to make your acquaintance and have been following your exploits since the disappearance of Gregory Hines. I suspect you were responsible for that as you were responsible for the ultimate end of Victor Corbinelli. I admire those who strive to make their communities a better place, as you have done. I will be in the city soon, and I hope to meet. You and I have much in common, and I have ideas I would like to share with you. Sincerely, Damien Hartwell."

She set the letter on the table after rattling off the phone number beneath his signature.

Rowan and Ethan stood beside each other, arms folded. Rowan's face was as grim as usual, but Ethan raised a brow. "Do you know a Damien Hartwell?"

Stacy replied, "I've met a lot of people, but I don't remember hearing that name before."

"Well, he seems to know *you*," Ethan remarked. "I want to know what he meant by, 'You and I have a lot in common.'"

"Me too." Stacy sat down and ran her hands from her thighs to her knees.

"What I want to know," Rowan growled, "is how and why he has watched you since Gregory Hines. No one but our inner circle knows what truly happened there."

"For that matter, only our circle knows what truly happened with Victor," Ethan added. As far as everyone knew, Victor's estate had caught fire and burned down, and he had died in the flames. That was true, but few knew that Stacy had caused the fire in dragon form. Better that way.

Did this Damien person know? Was he a paranormal too? What the hell did he want with her? "I'll call this number in the morning and see what this is about." Stacy gestured at the letter.

"Allow me," Rowan cut in. He took the letter off the table and put it back in the envelope. Stacy shot him an appreciative smile. Empty takeout boxes still littered the table. After they had thanked Miles for bringing it to them and filled their stomachs, they had turned their attention to the letter.

Miles, who was chucking garbage into a can on the other side of the kitchen, spoke next. "I figure this fella wants in on the action. Your reputation has probably spread farther than the city by now, Stacy. Probably outside the state."

Stacy didn't like that idea. "'In on the action?'"

Miles nodded. "He wants a taste of your power. Sidle up to the big guy."

Stacy rolled her eyes. "I don't want to be the 'big guy.' Do you think this Damien is under the impression that I'm…I don't know, the queen of the underworld?"

Miles shrugged. "Could be. You'll have to meet him to find out."

Stacy didn't want to waste her time, but she was curious. She turned to Rowan. "Please call him in the morning and see what he wants. If he's in town, we can meet at my father's estate."

"Not here?" Ethan asked.

Stacy shook her head. "This is our home, and I would rather no one know that anyone lives here. Plus, my dad's place is more intimidating." She smirked.

Rowan nodded curtly. "I will do that first thing."

Stacy leaned back in the chair, sighing. "Amy should be back tomorrow. I will ask her to look into his background. I would do it myself, but I have—"

"A million other things to do?" Ethan inserted.

She nodded, running down the list in her mind: remove gang leaders and drug lords, train the witches in her coven, and keep her estates running. Before, the anticipation of entering a courtroom had been enough excitement for her. "I hope meeting this Damien Hartwell guy won't be a waste of time. I can't afford that right now."

The sound of someone crunching into an apple reached her ears, followed by the muffled words, "You have plans?"

Stacy turned to Miles. "I want to go see my father's other estates around the country and determine which ones are worth keeping and what to sell. I plan to take Amy with me, and some of the Graytails might come too, so we can get into touch with local packs who might need more land."

"Or negotiate terms with packs who use your father's land while he's away," Rowan stated.

Stacy hadn't thought about that. She motioned at the letter in Rowan's hand. "Do you think I should alert my father about that?"

Rowan shook his head. "Not yet. We don't know what is going to come of this. For all we know, Damien could just be a paranormal fanatic who wants your attention. If it gets serious, then reach out to your father."

Stacy wanted to use it as a reason to talk to him, but she needed to prove she could handle anything that came her way. He had enough to deal with.

Miles clapped his hands and moved toward the freezer. "Now for dessert! How does ice cream sound?"

CHAPTER FOUR

The thrum of the motorcycle's engine beneath Kiera's body never got old. She wound down country roads toward the Thorn estate, having left the city and her nighttime exploits behind. It felt good to be the only person on the road. The night wind pierced her, but Kiera liked it. She knew every curve in this road since she had traversed it a hundred times.

Look at me. Never thought I'd stay in one place this long.

She had Stacy to thank for that, as well as Rowan and Miles. She couldn't believe she trusted someone with the wealth and status Stacy Drakethorn had or that she was friends with Miles Ironwood again. Most of all, that she'd allowed herself to fall in love with Rowan again. What now? she wondered. Kiera couldn't imagine leaving.

Her gloved hands tightened on the handlebars as she took a sharp curve, cutting close to the tall grass on the side of the road and the trees only a few feet away. Stacy had given her the Ducati as a birthday gift. It was one of the best bikes on the market and Kiera's most prized possession after her daggers. She'd told Stacy it was too much, but her friend had insisted that since she had a nice ride, everyone would. "Besides, you're my primo 'errand runner,' Kiera," she'd added.

As Kiera drove, she considered the trouble the young man had gone through to find her. She wondered if something beyond gratitude for Stacy was in play. Had the person who'd given him the note threatened or bribed him? And he had seen the body, though not the face, so he could not identify him. Kiera hadn't regretted any of her missions, but she didn't want the kills traced to Stacy.

Kiera was drowsy despite the adrenaline from the encounter. It was past midnight. The clouds had moved to reveal the full glory of the moon for most of the drive. *Almost there,* she told herself. *Then bed.* She imagined Rowan waiting for her with a cup of Earl Grey tea and curling into his arms after she showered and changed.

The clouds moved over the moon as someone exploded from the trees on the side of the road and slammed into her. Her bike's tires screeched, and Kiera hit the concrete with a groan. If not for her helmet, she would have scraped her face. The bike fell on top of her, pinning her to the asphalt. *Fuck!*

What was that? Couldn't have been an animal. Too fast.

Pain flared in several parts of her body. Kiera tried to lever the bike off, but one of her arms was pinned too, and the hand was going numb. People stood over her, indistinguishable thanks to hoods concealing their faces. Her helmet had popped off when she hit the road, revealing her face and the black braid twisting down past her breasts.

One of her attackers hauled the bike off as another yanked her up. Kiera threw her elbow back to hit him in the gut, but the point of her elbow hit something hard. Armor. *Double fuck.*

The man holding her chuckled.

Kiera reached for her dagger, but her hand had barely grazed the hilt when her wrist was snatched away. Another man drew the dagger free and held it up in the moonlight, laughing. "No more pretty daggers for you, princess." He tossed it into the trees. A snarl ripped through Kiera's throat, but she didn't get any words out. She lurched for the male who'd thrown her dagger but was jerked back, and someone shoved cloth into her mouth. There were four of them. Otherwise, she could have taken them.

Four humans would have been easy, but these people were not human. They were…

Fuck. Kiera's heart sank. It couldn't be. How?

Thoughts rattled through her head, each more dreadful than the last. Kiera went to summon her magic, but her body got very heavy. *I've been fucking drugged!* It wasn't a human-made drug either, but a magical one. It had to be, given how quickly it worked. Her mind was muddled, and her head felt full of cement. Kiera struggled to stay conscious. *I have to…get…free. Get…away…*

The words jumbled in her mind, and her moan was trapped in her throat. Everything hurt. Then a thought came, as clear and sharp as one of her daggers. Kiera had thought the male's epithet "princess" was an insult, but these people apparently knew she was really a princess. Those taking *her* down could only be fae.

She could barely string thoughts together. Her people didn't come to the human world. She was one of a very few who'd come here long ago, and only because she'd been banished. Why were they here now?

Those were her last thoughts as darkness claimed her.

"Maybe he has a crush on you," Ethan teased as he climbed into bed.

Stacy, standing by her dresser, turned and frowned. "I doubt that."

Ethan shrugged. "I do, so I wouldn't blame the guy if he did."

Stacy unclasped her mother's locket and set it on the dresser before sauntering over to the bed, swishing her hips to give

Ethan the full effect of the lacy pajama set. She'd bought it for his pleasure. His eyes roved up her body, meeting her eyes last. A smile touched his lips. "You're not wearing that to your meeting tomorrow, are you?"

"Jealous?" she cooed as she dropped onto the bed.

Ethan glowered. "If you wear that, I will be."

Stacy swatted his arm. "If I walked into my father's house wearing something as skimpy as this, Regi would have a heart attack. I will be decent and professional, and it doesn't matter if he has a crush on me. I have you." She looped Ethan's arm across her shoulders and nestled into the blankets and pillows.

Ethan kissed her temple and put his other arm behind his head. He looked good lying there, shirtless and relaxed. "That letter was strange. I can't stop thinking about it."

Stacy drew circles on the palm of his hand. "We've been to hell and back. People who come to us wanting something usually don't want anything good."

She thought about several witches they had interviewed who'd wanted nothing more than to be close to her, dig out her secrets, and sell them to the highest bidder. In recent weeks, she'd seen wild rumors about her printed in the New York Times. Journalists had written the articles without interviewing her, not that she would have accepted.

In one, she was rumored to be marrying a prince from Dubai. In another, she was pregnant with the governor of California's baby. She'd never even met the governor of California. Unauthorized photos splashed front pages, edited to make her look thinner or heavier than she was.

"Lots of journalists are scumbags," Amy had told her. "Ignore what the tabloids write, and *fuck* that NYT guy."

Stacy thought about her coven. So far, their new members had been good fits. Only time would tell if they were in it for the long-term, however. They had not yet met any disasters or true tests of loyalty and determination, but those would come upon them sooner or later.

"Are you okay?" Ethan murmured, seeing the thoughts churning behind the green eyes that were so much like her father's.

Stacy nodded. "Just thinking."

Ethan turned on his side and surveyed her face. "You worry too much."

Stacy gazed at him. "*You* were worrying if the man who sent me a mysterious letter has romantic feelings for me, and I've never met him."

Ethan chuckled and pressed his lips to her neck. Stacy arched. "Oh!"

"You worry too much," he murmured onto her skin.

Stacy took his face and directed his lips to hers. After the kiss, he asked, "Did you ever think you would fall in love with the man teaching you magic?"

Stacy laughed. "I didn't. Did you think you would fall in love with the woman who stumbled into your bookshop?"

He shook his head, tickling her with his hair.

"How lucky am I?" she murmured.

Ethan winked. "Very lucky." He kissed her again. Stacy leaned over to the nightstand to switch off the lamp and hoped none of the sprites would wander into the room tonight as Ethan's warm hand drifted over her stomach, lifting the camisole.

Ethan's lips went to her ear, his warm breath caressing her. "I hope Kiera is back by breakfast and we get to eat pastries."

A laugh bubbled out of Stacy's throat. "Let's not talk about that now."

"Let's not talk at all."

Rowan sat in his study with the letter from Damien Hartwell open on his lap. A lamp on the desk lit the room. Rowan's eyes were fixed on a distant point, his fist supporting his chin. He did not move until he heard movement in the doorway. He turned to see Miles ambling in, hands deep in his gardening trousers.

"It's late, Miles."

"It is," the groundskeeper agreed. "Don't give me a speech about going to bed. You're still up, too. Waiting for Kiera?"

"She doesn't usually get back until dawn. I will see her in the morning." In bed, hopefully, warm and pressed close. How he had gone all those years without her, he did not know.

Miles took the other leather armchair by the desk and surveyed Rowan's grim expression. "Don't worry so much, Rowan." He gestured at the letter. "Stacy will handle it like she always does."

The dryad sighed and put the letter on the desk. "I'm not worried about that. I only wish I could take more off her plate. I would hate to see her break from the weight she carries." The distant look in his eyes told Miles that Rowan had seen that happen once, not to Stacy but to her mother.

Infiltrating the underworld and trying to bring justice and light to those dark, festering places in the city had been too much for Catherine Thorn, despite having Khan at her side and a daughter growing in her womb. Rowan regretted that he had not done more to help her.

Miles chuckled. "Stacy will be the last to break, trust me. Besides, our plates are piled high too." His face got somber. "We've come a long way, haven't we? Once, we were on war-torn battlefields, swinging axes and watching our friends die. Now look at us! We live on a quiet estate in the countryside, working for a golden-hearted heiress."

That didn't mean their lives were uneventful. They'd encountered plenty of danger and excitement since moving here—especially Rowan, who'd come decades before his friends had. They were much better off in this place, and it had brought the three of them back together and healed the old wounds between them.

Images of those years on battlefields swept through his mind: blood soaking the ground, bodies everywhere, stalking through the gory mud. He saw Miles bent over an old friend, tears flowing from his eyes, Kiera standing nearby like a wavering shadow. Those days were well behind them, and Rowan hoped they would never see the like again.

A faint smile came to his lips. "Our lives have turned out well."

CHAPTER FIVE

Stacy awoke before Ethan and shuffled out of the room without a sound. Downstairs, she heard the coffee machine grinding in the kitchen, the scent of beans wafting into the hallway. She expected to find Kiera there, putting the finishing touches on breakfast before going to bed. Instead, Stacy saw a golden-haired young woman selecting a carton of cream from the refrigerator.

"Amy! I didn't think you would be back this early."

Amy turned, smiling. "I got in late last night. Everyone except Rowan was in bed."

Stacy hugged her friend before lowering herself onto one of the kitchen chairs. Golden sunlight streamed through the window, making the old wooden floorboards glow. Outside, the trees were shedding the last of their leaves, blanketing the ground in browns, reds, and oranges. Miles would have a good time raking and piling today. Sprites danced across the windowsill or flitted about the coffee machine, enjoying the scents as much as the women did. "How was your trip?"

"It went smoothly. It was a charming village. I wish I could have stayed longer." The journalist poured a mug of coffee, then another for Stacy. Both mugs had come from Stacy's apartment.

One said *Allegedly*, and another said, *See you in court, bitch*. Both had been gifts from her friend Jenny during their first year at the law firm. Rowan hated the mugs, but Stacy would not part with them, so into the cupboard they'd gone.

Amy sat across from Stacy, palming the mug as she brought it to her lips. After determining the liquid was still too hot, she set it down. Steam wafted into her face as she continued, "I have photographs of both men, and I'll be working on the article this week."

Stacy nodded. "Thank you for all your hard work, Amy."

Amy leaned back in the chair, seeming tired. "I saw Rowan when I got in. He was in a quiet mood, which can only mean something's up. What happened while I was away?"

"Nothing major. Not yet, anyway." Stacy told her friend about the letter she'd received last night.

Amy arched a brow when she finished and brought her mug to her lips again. "Sounds like an interesting guy. Ethan might be right; maybe he does have a crush on you."

"Or maybe he's gay, and he'll have a crush on Rowan," Stacy suggested.

Amy chuckled. "Everyone has a crush on Rowan."

"What are you saying about me?" the dryad asked as he strode into the kitchen.

"Oh, nothing," Amy chirped.

Rowan shot Stacy a questioning look. "Anything to report?" she asked him.

"Yes. I called Damien Hartwell's assistant, and we arranged a lunch meeting at your father's estate today. Apparently, Mr. Hartwell is in the city. He must have written and sent that letter before coming here, and it arrived after he did. I checked your schedule, and you have nothing until this afternoon."

"Perfect," Stacy replied.

"I called Reginald and informed him, too. He promised us Esme's best lunch spread," Rowan added.

Stacy thanked Rowan, then turned to Amy. "I would like you to research Damien Hartwell while we're at the meeting. That way, when we get back, we can corroborate what he says about himself."

"Aye aye, Captain!"

Rowan winced at her volume. Stacy grinned. Miles was worse, and he would be down soon.

Stacy glanced at Rowan. "Is Kiera in bed?"

Rowan shook his head. "Kiera isn't back, and she hasn't sent word as to what is delaying her. Sometimes, the people she has to track down end up being bigger messes than she anticipates. I'm not concerned yet."

"Well, I look forward to seeing her when she's back." Amy stood and stretched her arms over her head before claiming that she had to go upstairs and unpack.

"And I have to get ready for our meeting," Stacy told Rowan. "We should drive over shortly before noon."

The car rumbled over the gravel drive, past the grand wrought iron fence surrounding her father's estate. *My estate*, Stacy reminded herself. Despite having grown up here and her father having formally handed over the management of this place, it did not feel like it belonged to her.

Stacy knew every turn of the driveway, every path through the back gardens, every window and corridor inside the house. She had it memorized like the lines in her hand, and yet she still felt intimidated coming up to the house. It swallowed her whole and reminded her that her legacy was much larger than it sometimes felt. The estate felt like home and an otherworldly place at the same time.

It amused her to think about how Damien Hartwell would feel when he arrived. If she was swallowed by her childhood home, he might feel as though he were walking into the yawning mouth of some great, hungry beast. Perhaps that was what Khan had wanted when he built the house.

"Are you ready?" Rowan pulled up to the front of the house and put the car in park. They had the windows rolled up, but the November chill pressed against the glass.

"I'm ready. It's not knowing what he wants that's killing me," Stacy admitted.

Rowan gave her an encouraging smile. "Regardless, we get to enjoy Esme's cooking."

He was right. Rowan alighted first and came around to her side to open the door. Stacy would have opened it herself, but Rowan insisted on following "proper protocol." Stacy noticed he did that more when Reginald Blackguard was watching. A staff member came toward them as Stacy's boots touched the gravel drive. Rowan handed him the keys, murmuring instructions. The man nodded, and Stacy and Rowan headed toward the porch.

The front door opened before Stacy and Rowan reached it, and Stacy felt like a child coming to visit her grandfather. Reginald stood in the doorway wearing a kind smile. He spread his arms. "Good to see you, Miss Anastasia." He nodded a greeting to Rowan, who returned the gesture.

"All is well here, I trust?" Stacy asked as she stepped into the hallway. Reginald took her gray wool coat and hung it on a hook. Stacy wore plain dark jeans and a black turtleneck. Her auburn hair was up in a bun, bangs brushing her neatly arched eyebrows. Rowan wore beige trousers and a pale green sweater. He seemed unbothered by the temperature outside.

"All is well," Reginald assured her as he closed the front door. "Torin went to a gardening fair down south but will return tomorrow. Esme is in the kitchen putting the final touches on your lunch."

Stacy smiled warmly. "Good to hear. I hope Torin is enjoying himself."

Reginald pursed his lips, locking his white-gloved hands behind his back. "Too much, probably." Stacy chuckled, then stepped around him to visit the library/study. Rowan lingered to discuss estate matters. As guardians of their respective manors, they had much to converse about. Stacy left them to it.

Stacy could not bring herself to change anything in the house, especially this room. The shelves were full of old, dusty books bound in leather or cloth. Others were preserved by magic and stored in secret compartments or trunks. Khan's huge desk was covered with trinkets and artifacts from his past, each carrying a tale.

Stacy traced the edge of the desk, gazing at her father's favorite inkwell and quill pen. She smiled. He was so old-fashioned sometimes. In contrast, a widescreen TV adorned the opposite wall. He had often watched his favorite soap operas while enjoying Chinese takeout. Above a fireplace was a painting of him and Catherine in front of an arched window upstairs that overlooked the estate. Mornings, sunlight flooded through that window. Stacy remembered lying on the floorboards, basking in the sun until someone came up and shooed her to her feet.

Stacy perused the bookshelves, but her eyes strayed to the windows overlooking the garden. At this time of year, nearly everything was dormant, but the sight gave Stacy comfort. The whole estate did.

I won't change anything anytime soon, she decided. *I hope Dad pops in.* Khan would be perturbed if he came home and found the décor changed despite having handed its management over to his daughter. Six weeks of not being able to stop by and see him anytime she wanted had felt like an eternity. To Khan, it had probably felt like a week. He *was* centuries old.

Will I feel like that one day? Stacy wondered. Would she outlive her friends? Amy was human, and Ethan was a witch. He would live longer than most people, but not as long as she would. Rowan, Kiera, and Miles had been alive for centuries. *None of us are mortal, and we could all die of things unrelated to old age*, Stacy reminded herself. The thought sobered her, so she sought a window to overlook the grounds.

Someone at the study's door cleared their throat. She turned to see Reginald standing there with a smile. "Lunch is ready, Miss Anastasia, and your guest has arrived."

Damien Hartwell was standing in the hallway, having been admitted by Reginald. Stacy approached with the butler beside her as Rowan came out of the dining room, his green eyes sweeping from Stacy to the new arrival.

Damien wasn't what Stacy had expected.

He was a tad taller than her, not quite six feet, and had broad shoulders and a square, chiseled face. Dark brown curls were brushed back from his face, where a proud brow and lips were the most prominent features. His brown eyes wandered the hallway, taking in the framed paintings, photographs, and artifacts Khan had on display, ranging from ancient battle horns preserved by magic to rusting weaponry and armor to teeth belonging to... Stacy didn't quite know. Wild animals, once-great foes, or vampires? Could be any of those or something more fantastical.

When he heard the floor creak, Damien turned his attention to the mistress of the house and the two men accompanying her. Damien wore a tan tweed sports coat and beige slacks, with a loose green tie and brown loafers. The colors suited him and gave him an air of old money and tradition. He looked like he had attended an Ivy League school, not an FBI agent who'd somehow learned of her deeper connection to Corbinelli and Hines.

The man wasn't impressive until he smiled. Then he radiated

charisma and success. Maybe it was better Ethan wasn't here. Stacy smothered her amusement as she approached him.

"Ms. Drakethorn," Damien greeted, his voice like oil. He dipped his head. "Thank you for arranging this meeting so quickly. I heard about your discipline and promptness, but I am still impressed."

Stacy smiled as she took Damien's extended hand and firmly shook it. "A pleasure to meet you, Mr. Hartwell. Please call me Stacy. I trust your trip here went well?"

"Only if you call me Damien." His eyes glittered. "My trip was smooth, thank you. I have an estate not far outside DC, but I have been in New York City for the past few days. I hope to be here for the rest of the week."

Stacy gestured at Reginald, then Rowan. "You have already met this estate's butler and manager Reginald Blackguard. This is Rowan, my bodyguard, driver, and caretaker."

Rowan gave Damien a curt nod in greeting.

Damien returned the dryad's intent stare. "Ah, yes. My assistant said she spoke to someone named Rowan. What is your last name, sir?"

"It's just Rowan," the dryad replied.

Reginald cleared his throat. "Miss Anastasia, Esme says lunch is ready."

Stacy smiled at Damien. "I hope you're hungry. My cook is spectacular."

Damien's lips twitched. "I will take your word for it, Stacy."

Despite Stacy having asked him to address her by her first name, Rowan bristled. Reginald departed, leaving Stacy and Rowan to lead Damien to the dining room. "In the spring and summer, we take lunch in the garden. It's too cold for that today," Stacy told their guest. "We will have to admire the grounds from here."

Esme had opened the curtains in the normally dim dining room. The sun flooded in, illuminating the frost that limned the panes. Stacy surmised that it might snow tonight. She took the seat at the head of the table where her father usually sat. It felt right in his absence. Rowan sat to her right, and Damien took the spot across from him.

"This house is marvelous, Stacy, as are the grounds." Damien's gaze met hers. "It reminds me of my home."

"Does it?" she asked as she unfolded a napkin and placed it on her lap.

"Yes. The Hartwell estate has many gardens as well as a stocked fishing lake. It's small, but it does the job. We have room for hunting and all sorts of sports. My father liked anything out of doors." Damien seemed to enjoy speaking of his home.

Stacy shot Rowan a look that said, *"He seems nice so far."*

Rowan's expression gave away nothing. Later, then.

"I have long wondered what the Drakethorn estate would look like," Damien added. "It is more magnificent than I imagined."

He'd heard about this place? Interesting, although Khan was too wealthy and influential and involved in the affairs of New York City not to be known in limited circles. The trio turned their attention to the food. Esme had prepared a pot roast with every vegetable imaginable, all grown in greenhouses that Torin kept warm with magic during the colder months. The cook used home-grown herbs as well.

Esme had also made an assortment of rolls and biscuits. The trio passed the dishes, scooping food onto their plates. A moment later, Esme bustled into the dining room, wiping her hands on her white apron. "Hello, Stacy dear. It's good to see you." She bent to kiss Stacy's cheek.

"Everything looks and smells delicious, Esme. Thank you."

Esme tutted. "It's no problem. I was glad to hear you were coming today. I don't often get to make so much food!"

Damien, who'd been preparing a bite of roast, paused, his

keen eyes sweeping over the woman. After Esme had left the room, he asked, "Are you not often here?"

Stacy did not wish to tell him she spent most of her time elsewhere. She just smiled warmly. "I have an apartment in the city." It was true, though she seldom spent time there. It was for Amy and Kiera when they had late-night jobs in the city and didn't want to drive home. Stacy wondered if Kiera was there now, resting after a long night, too tired to come home when she was finished.

Before Damien could inquire further, Rowan inserted himself. It was the first time he had spoken since they came into the dining room. "Mr. Hartwell, would you please tell us why you sent the letter? A phone call or email would have sufficed."

Stacy shot Rowan a warning look.

Damien chuckled sheepishly, wiping the corners of his mouth with a napkin. "I know how it looks, and I apologize for both that and the vagueness of the letter. I'm sure it caused you concern. I did it because I did not want any of your enemies finding out about us connecting. I understand you have had many difficult people rise against you in the city, and I did not want to worsen the problem by making it obvious we were meeting."

How did he know that? Did the FBI know too?

Stacy put her elbows on the table and rested her chin on her interlocked fingers. "Are you here as a representative of the FBI or for your own curiosity?"

Damien laughed. "My curiosity. My colleagues don't know." He leaned forward too, keeping his focus on Stacy while ignoring Rowan's intent stare. The dryad hadn't touched his food. "We have much in common, Stacy. That is why I am so interested in you. We were both raised in large houses as only children to men with great legacies. Both heirs to those homes and the vast resources our fathers left us."

Did Damien know her father was not here? Where did he think Khan was?

Stacy realized she should have thought this through better. It might have been wiser to meet in the city instead of her father's estate since Constantine Drakethorn was clearly not in residence right now.

Damien continued, his shoulders relaxed and his smile easy. Words flowed off his tongue with an ease that made Stacy wonder if he'd rehearsed the story. "My father never stopped working or lost sight of his goals, so I didn't see much of him growing up. I was surrounded by tutors and servants." His laugh seemed forced.

A lonely childhood. Stacy related to that on some level. She hadn't known many people her age while growing up. Some of her past tutors had had children she'd spent time with, but otherwise, she'd not had friends her age until she left for college.

"My mother was always there, though." Damien's eyes turned sad. "Until she ran away. She died before I turned eighteen, succumbing to mental illness. I understand you also lost your mother."

Stacy could have sworn she heard the table groan as Rowan put his arms on it. "Catherine Thorn died shortly after Stacy's birth due to health complications. It wasn't the same."

"You knew her," Damien observed. "I am sorry."

"And I am sorry to hear about your mother," Stacy inserted, shooting Rowan a reproving look. He was right. Damien's story was not the same as hers, but the dryad didn't have to use that tone.

Damien cleared his throat. "I only said that because our mothers were both witches."

Stacy had not expected to hear that. Even Rowan arched a brow. "But in her case, the magic meddled with her mind," Damien added with a sigh. "Neither my father nor I knew about it until she left. We found her spell books and journals, odd scribblings that didn't make sense."

Because she'd been crazy or because the books had been

written in a magical language they didn't know? Stacy considered spells in her mother's journals that had required translation. With Ethan and Rowan's help, she had been able to understand and use them.

"My father died several years ago of age and illness," Damien went on. "It was difficult to let him go, but he was suffering. I am glad he is in pain no more."

Damien Hartwell seemed like a very lonely person. Stacy glanced at his left hand but saw no ring. Not married, then. Probably no children, either. "I do wonder why you work for the FBI," she spoke up. "You don't have to, assuming your father left you everything he had."

Damien gave her a knowing smile that was softer than the grins he'd displayed before. "I am like you, Stacy. I want to make a difference and help others."

His words didn't seem genuine, but Stacy didn't let him see that. Before she could reply, he added, "I heard a lot about what you have done for the city and the people in the surrounding area. I think the world could use more people like you, Stacy Drakethorn."

She arched a brow. "What do you mean, Damien Hartwell?"

"Well, you're a dragon, for one." The matter-of-fact tone in which he said that made her pause. He spoke this as if it were obvious.

"Come on, Stacy," Damien continued. "I know what you are. You and your father. As I said, the world needs better leadership, and the dragons have led from the shadows beyond the veil for centuries. Perhaps it is time for dragons to lead in the light now."

Stacy took his words in. She sensed something amiss, like she was descending stairs in the dark and missed one, nearly hurtling down the rest. "What are you, Damien?"

Damien sighed. "Though my mother was a witch, my father was human. I inherited none of my mother's magic as far as I can tell." Not a paranormal, then. Still, he had power and influence not only in his FBI position but due to his wealthy family's history. Stacy hoped to learn more about that from Amy's research.

Damien was too old to awaken his magic now. He went on. "The FBI has long been aware of your father and his true nature, Stacy, and now we are aware of yours." Did he know how she'd brought down Victor and Hines?

"I can help you with some of your problems," Damien continued. "Given my standing in the FBI and your abilities in the courts of law, I propose that we work together toward a better future." He had cleared his plate and now drained his glass of water. "I will be returning to DC soon, but you are welcome to come to my office to discuss ideas at any time." He smiled again. "Or better yet, come to my home, as you have so graciously invited me to your father's."

Not hers. Khan's. He knew.

Fuck.

Stacy pasted a smile to her lips. "You have presented your case well. I'm surprised that you are interested in working with me, but I am open to the idea. Rowan will give you my office number, and we will be in touch."

Rowan looked like he wanted to grumble, "Please don't make me," but he kept his mouth shut. Their lunch was soon over, and Damien claimed he must head back to the city for work. Rowan remained in the dining room to help Esme clear the dishes while Stacy walked Damien to the front door.

Before she opened it, he took her hand and bent to kiss it. "It's been a pleasure to meet you. I look forward to our next lunch." He straightened, winking. "And you look very nice today."

Stacy didn't know what to say, but it didn't matter since Damien took his hat and coat off their hooks and disappeared through the door. The attendant had brought his car around. Stacy watched him drive to the gate.

Rowan appeared behind her, arms folded. "He was interesting."

CHAPTER SIX

"You can tell me how you feel now, Rowan." They were in the car, heading back to her estate. The dryad gripped the steering wheel harder than normal. "The food upset your stomach?" Stacy teased.

"Never. Esme's cooking is always delicious." He shot her a look. "Don't tell Kiera I said that."

"Then what is it?"

Rowan considered his words. "I didn't see anything wrong with the man, but he was as vague in his speech as he was in the letter."

Was he? Stacy wondered. Damien had spoken openly about his life and the hardships he'd been through.

"He spoke broadly of his plans and interest in you," Rowan elaborated. "He gave no particulars on ways you could work together. Did he mean legally or communally in terms of business and real estate?"

Stacy assumed it was legally since he was with the FBI. Then again, Damien had given no specifics and claimed his interest in her had nothing to do with the agency. Rowan was right.

"I'm just wary," Rowan finished. "Be cautious, Stacy. That's my advice."

She gave him an appreciative smile. "I will, Rowan. Thank you."

Not long after, he drove them through the gate of the Thorn estate, dropping her at the door before he rounded the house to park it in the garage. Stacy went inside and found Amy and Miles in the dining room, enjoying egg salad sandwiches and homemade tortilla chips with Miles' favorite salsa. Stacy hoped Amy had researched Damien and found things that would help them. Amy was bent over a laptop, scrutinizing the screen as Miles hummed between crunches.

Amy glanced at Stacy. "How did it go?"

"I had a different experience than Rowan." Stacy laughed, then shared what had happened and all that Damien had said.

Amy nodded along, looking thoughtful. "Everything he told you matches what I have found so far. FBI employment, house and family, age. He has not married or had children, though he's had a slew of model girlfriends."

Stacy recalled the flirtatious comment he'd made before he left. It hit her that he had waited to say that when Rowan wasn't around. "What about the public? What do people think about him?"

"There's not much out there about Damien, but a lot of people hated his father." Amy leaned back, closing her laptop and rubbing her eyes. "Apparently, James Hartwell was known in the DC area as 'Slimy Jimmy,' often making underhanded real estate deals and impeding the commercial successes of people who had called him friend. Many considered him to be a greedy prick, and by the time of his death, he had few allies left. I imagine Damien was one of the few people at his funeral."

Miles shook his head. "That's sad."

She shrugged. "That's what my research says."

Stacy's picture of Damien as a lonely man increased with

Amy's words. "Anything on his mother? I was surprised to learn she was a witch."

"Actually, that's the weirdest part. Annabelle Carter Hartwell was a pretty and quiet woman, always on her husband's arm at galas and events. Tons of pictures online. One day, she snapped, seemingly out of the blue. The neighbors said she ran away, jabbering about how cruel and violent her husband was. No one imagined that she would leave her son, but she did. She was found dead in a forest in Tennessee several months later. They claimed it was suicide."

Damien had not discussed that, but Stacy didn't blame him. Meeting someone for the first time did not entail spilling your trauma. Amy cited her sources as being neighbors who had been interviewed both for news articles and on TV, as well as the law enforcement officers who had discovered her body.

"I feel like there's more to the story," Amy concluded. "I'll see what else I can find. For now, that's it."

Stacy asked if she had photos of the Hartwell estate. Amy showed her the images she'd found. It was a grand old place built of stone with the gardens and lake he had mentioned. "Speaking of estates," Amy said, "weren't you going to visit some of your father's soon?"

Stacy smiled. "I am. We could go to the one in Pennsylvania first. It's the closest."

"We don't have a lot of time," Amy reminded her.

Stacy's green eyes glowed with flecks of gold. "I know a way to get there faster."

"I don't like your tone, Stacy. It sounds like you're scheming."

"I'm not scheming!"

"Sounds like it," Miles agreed as he licked yogurt off a spoon.

"As long as you're not afraid of heights, you'll be fine," Stacy told Amy.

"What's going on?" Rowan asked as he came into the room.

Amy cast her eyes on him. "Stacy wants me to ride her as a dragon!"

Rowan chuckled. "Sounds fun."

"Sounds fucking cold," Miles mumbled.

"You can wear a coat!" Stacy declared.

Rowan changed the subject. "We will discuss it later. Ethan is in your office with Clara Stoneward. She arrived for her interview."

Stacy had forgotten about the interview. With everything going on, the coven had slipped onto the back burner.

If she didn't expand the coven, how could they see her as a good leader? At this point, Ethan was carrying more weight than she was.

Stacy hurried through the garden toward the cottage she had converted into an office. Rowan lovingly referred to it as her "computer shed" despite it being quite large, but then, Rowan called the eight-bedroom house a cottage. When she stepped in, Ethan was sitting behind her desk, though not in her chair. He had dragged a stool over. A young woman with mousy brown hair braided down her back sat on the opposite side of the desk, hands folded in her lap.

Stacy rounded the desk to take her seat, smiling at the young woman. Clara was no more than twenty. The coven had a range of ages and backgrounds, but none were as young as this person. "Clara, thank you for coming. We're glad to talk to you today and see if you're a good fit."

Clara smiled warmly. Her eyes were a light gray-blue that matched her wool sweater. Her dark blue jeans had tiny butterflies embroidered in several places. Stacy wondered if she'd applied them herself. "Thank you, Ms. Drakethorn. You have a lovely home. My father said you did. He's never been here, but Rowan has told him about this place."

"I asked Clara about how she knows Rowan," Ethan chimed in.

"He and my father have been friends for years," Clara explained. "My father says he met your mother too."

Stacy smiled. "That's wonderful to hear." She folded her hands. "Tell me how old you are and why you are interested in joining our coven."

The girl was shy, but she spoke clearly and without faltering. "I turned eighteen a month ago, Miss Drakethorn."

"Please, call me Stacy."

Clara smiled, her cheeks tinged pink. "I have been a witch for as long as I can remember. My father has been teaching me, and he thinks I am ready to use my skills in a coven. He has been concerned joining a random coven would not be safe for me, considering the circumstances we witches usually find ourselves in."

Ethan nodded, his expression solemn.

"What about your mother?" Stacy asked.

"She died when I was young. I don't remember much about her, but she was a witch too."

Stacy was sympathetic. She had the sense that Clara's story was like Damien's and that Clara had led a lonely life. In this case, however, Stacy heard no alarm bells. "I am sorry to hear that. My mother died when I was a baby, as I am sure you know from your father."

Clara nodded. "I want to help others and make a difference. Like you, Ms....I mean, Stacy."

Stacy smiled. "I can tell."

Ethan asked a slew of questions to probe Clara's knowledge of magic. To their surprise, Clara was very advanced. The only skill she lacked was working with multiple witches. "My father and I have done much together, but I have never performed rituals with other witches," she admitted. She was quick to add, "But I'm a faster learner!"

Stacy believed her. "Ethan and I will talk it over, but you are a promising fit from what I have seen for far. Give us a few days to come to a decision."

Ethan offered Clara an encouraging nod. "You did well today. I will walk you back to your car."

Stacy waited in the office until Ethan ambled back in with his hands in his pockets.

He stated, "I don't know about you, but I liked her. She knows more than any witch her age I have ever met. She might lack experience in working with others, but her knowledge of arcane history far surpasses most of the witches in our coven. I think she will make an excellent addition and fit in well."

He sat on the stool once more, surveying Stacy's face. "You don't think so?"

"Everything you said is true," Stacy replied. "I only worry that she is too innocent. If she aligns herself with us, can she face the horrors we have dealt with?"

Seeing the worry on her face, Ethan scooted toward her and laid a comforting hand on her knee. "You're projecting what happened to Luna onto Clara, aren't you?"

Images flashed through Stacy's mind: the young werewolf's broken body, her solemn grave, the mourning pack. Voice tight, she said, "Maybe I am, but I don't want to be responsible for any other deaths."

"You weren't responsible for Luna's," he told her. "If anything, I was."

Stacy shook her head. "You weren't."

They lapsed into a glum silence, broken by Ethan squeezing her knee. "Clara has a strong moral compass, and that matters most. If the work is too much for her, we can give her other things to do until she is older and has seen more."

Stacy nodded. "That sounds good, and you're right. She will make an excellent addition."

Ethan smiled. "See? Our coven is coming along nicely. Your mother would be proud."

Stacy was grateful to hear that, though an ache bloomed in her chest. Ethan was right about their coven. They could become an unstoppable force for justice.

Maybe what Damien had said was right too. *Maybe someone like me should be in power.*

She banished the thought. Thinking that way would lead her down the wrong path.

The door opened, and Rowan's broad form filled the doorway. Stacy instantly knew something was wrong. Rowan was normally placid or grim. Right now, however, he was deeply concerned. "What's wrong?"

"I am concerned that Kiera hasn't returned yet or sent word. She should be back by now or called to let us know why she isn't." Rowan tried to keep his voice from shaking, imagining the worst.

Kiera was as capable as they came. Stacy couldn't imagine what could have gone wrong, but she nodded curtly. "If we haven't heard from her by nightfall, you should look for her. Take Miles with you."

Rowan nodded. "Thank you." After he left, Stacy looked at Ethan.

He hugged her. "Don't worry. Whatever happened, Kiera has it handled."

Stacy hoped that was true.

CHAPTER SEVEN

Damien tipped the decanter toward the glass and watched the amber liquid flow over the ice. When he raised the glass to his lips, his eyes roved through the windows overlooking New York City. The sun was setting, a thin glow of orange bleeding the last of its rays into the Upper Bay.

It felt strange to be so far from home. Damien was quite familiar with DC, though he was only there when he needed to be in the office. It was the Hartwell estate outside of DC where he felt at home. The bustle of this city made him nervous. Since he'd set foot here, Damien had felt high-strung. Going to the Drakethorn mansion earlier today had helped. It had felt good to breathe country air again.

Damien almost wished he cared about paranormals. He and Stacy really did have things in common, and he would have liked to become her friend if not for the matter of her bloodline. He'd told the truth when he said she looked nice today.

Damien pulled his mind away from Stacy and directed his attention across the city. From his hotel on the Upper East Side, Damien had a clear view of the Empire State Building as well as many other prominent skyscrapers.

The lights of the city spread out like twinkling diamonds. Damien wasn't like Victoria Corbinelli in the sense that he was not interested in sweeping the diamonds into his palm and keeping them. He had no interest in real estate or business. He simply wanted some of the people in the city to go away.

For good.

He considered all the paranormals blending in, slinking through the shadows. They hid in plain sight.

Like my mother did, Damien thought, his hand clenching the glass. What he'd told Stacy about not finding out she was a witch until after he died was true. His mother had felt the need to hide it from her husband.

Images flashed into Damien's mind: bruises on her wrists and neck and her gaunt, pale face. His father pretending to ignore her.

Damien downed the remainder of his drink. He had left out several details. Best not to scare her off by dumping his trauma on her. He already wondered if he had shared too much.

No, I said the perfect amount. He'd seen the sympathy in her eyes. She would come visit him. He was sure of it.

Damien tapped the side of the glass, the melting pieces of ice inside sliding about. The dryad might be a problem. Maybe it would be worth it to plant seeds in Stacy's mind that Rowan wasn't as loyal to her as he seemed. But how to do it? Damien would think of something.

Damien checked his watch. It was almost time for him to meet his contacts, all men once affiliated with Corbinelli or Hines. He'd recently heard about drug lords going missing or skipping town. Was Stacy responsible? Damien was all for that sort of scum being driven away or dealt with, but he didn't want paranormals replacing the human underlords.

There are paranormals in the underworld too, he reminded himself. That was another problem, but he decided to deal with them and the fae later.

Dread curled in the pit of Damien's stomach at the thought of the fae. He might have bitten off more than he could chew by striking the deal he had with the male who'd come to his home last week.

Damien lifted the glass to drink, then remembered he had finished it. He was on his way to pour another glass when there was a knock on his door. He frowned. Who could that be?

Damien set the glass down and walked past a luxurious king-sized bed, his open suitcase, and a muted TV. Damien opened to door to see a bellboy with a piece of paper on a thin metal tray. "Mr. Hartwell?"

"Yes?" Damien replied. The squeaky, freckled boy wore a uniform. Damien had removed his jacket and tie, unbuttoned his shirt at the top, and rolled the sleeves up to his elbows.

"A man came into the lobby and asked us to bring this up." The young man, no older than eighteen, extended the tray.

Damien took the paper. "Did he say what his name was?"

"No."

Damien closed the door and opened the note. All he saw was blank paper. He dug in his bag for a black light and shone it on the paper, revealing a short message written in crisp, perfect handwriting. It almost looked typed.

We have the fae princess Drakethorn employs. Waiting until she's conscious to question her. Stand by.

That would jumpstart his next step. He could meet his contacts tonight and let the fae take care of the bitch they had banished centuries ago, or so he'd been told.

Damien smiled. It didn't matter if Stacy chose to work with him since either way, her friends would die, starting with the fae assassin who'd taken out half her enemies in the city. Next would be the dryad. Damien didn't care who died after that.

"If she does work with me, it will be sweeter," he murmured

as he struck a match, lit the paper, and dropped it into a bagless trash can.

Kiera could only open one of her eyes, and that one was crusted with blood.

Her vision was blurred. She gauged how the rest of her body felt. Her head was throbbing, and the other eye was swollen shut. Pain sent sharp bolts through every tendon. Her limbs felt stiff and cold. It was worse than the chill she'd felt while riding through the countryside. This was not a piercing November wind promising winter but an empty, pervading coldness. She'd felt it before, but never in the human world.

The realization made her heart drop like a stone. *Fuck.*

Kiera noticed her arms were not at her sides. She was suspended in the air. She traced the chains around her wrists to anchors in the ceiling and the chains around her ankles to anchors in the floor. She felt as though one wrong move would tear her apart.

Kiera tried to push a groan past her lips, but her throat was too sore, and her lips were too dry to part more than a centimeter. Had she been screaming? It felt like it.

She could now see her surroundings: a stone wall with a closed wooden door in it, probably locked. The room was small and square, with no source of light except a torch on the left wall. *How medieval,* she thought. A patch of straw occupied one corner. It must have contained someone's feces, urine, or vomit since it smelled rank. Probably all three. She wondered who'd occupied this cell before her. At least she saw no bones.

Kiera was thirsty, hungry, and in a good deal of pain. What showed of her skin was crusted in dirt, blood, and sweat. Her cloak had been removed, leaving her in torn combat pants and her shirt.

How long had she been here? Where was she? Did it matter? The fae had come for her.

Everything rushed back: the attack on the road, a male throwing her dagger into the trees, and the magical drugs. Now she was a prisoner. This was not how her night was supposed to go.

Her only hope was that her friends would notice she was gone and had not been in contact. They would worry, and they could find her, but would it be too late? Kiera wasn't sure she was on the human world anymore. The fae might have hauled her ass back home.

No, it wasn't home. It was the shithole realm she'd been born in.

It was a green, prosperous land with bountiful rivers, many waterfalls, and sweet-smelling meadows. Humans could never dream of buildings such as the fae designed and giant trees far larger than the ones on Earth. What had made it a shithole was the tyrannical ruler she'd had to call Father. He'd called himself a king, but Kiera had hoped never to bow to him again. Not that doing so had been up to her.

A new fear rose within her. If Rowan and the others came to rescue her, even if they could find her, what if they got trapped? What if the fae overwhelmed them? Her kind were not beings to trifle with.

Kiera's ears perked up when boots scuffed on stone and low voices mingled beyond the door. Someone gave a rough laugh, and a key was inserted in the lock. Her heart lurched. She had not felt fear like this since…well, she'd last been on the fae world.

The door did not immediately open. One of the voices faded as boots shuffled down the corridor. One of the two had left. The door swung open on silent hinges and though she could not really focus, Kiera took in the fae who entered.

A male, perhaps one of those who'd brought her here. His smirk was evidence of that. His long hair was ebon-black and tightly braided, like Kiera's. She realized her hair wasn't in a braid anymore. They had taken it out and let her hair fall down her back.

Tendrils framed his beautiful face—beautiful because he was fae. They were all beautiful. It didn't stop Kiera from wanting to sink her dagger into him. If she could move, she'd wrap those chains around his neck and watch the breath leave his body.

The fae's skin was ivory, his eyes ice-blue. His smile was crooked, and his eyebrows were thick. He had the chiseled jawline of a god, and the figure of a warrior honed through centuries of conflict, so he was a solider in her father's court. *God. Fucking. Help. Me,* Kiera begged.

She took in the dagger on one hip and the sword on the other. He wasn't wearing armor, but the fighting leathers and flowing gold cape told her that her father hadn't changed his guards' uniforms. If not for the terror the fae invoked in anyone who saw them, the uniform would have looked like a silly costume. On Earth, they used glamours, hiding their otherworldly beauty and pointed ears.

Kiera did not recognize this guard. He must have come along after her rebellion with the assassin's guild and banishment to the human world. Perhaps he was the son of someone she'd known at court.

Kiera imagined what she looked like: roughed up, swollen eye, cuts covering her skin, torn clothes, and as defiant an expression as she could muster. Finally, the fae made a sound. He laughed.

Kiera froze.

"Well, isn't this a sight? The princess is strung up. I have waited a long time to see this." The hatred in his voice matched how Kiera felt toward him.

"Why did you bring me here?" she croaked. "I was b-banished." Getting words out wasn't easy.

"Silly princess, we didn't go back to our world. We're still on this festering shithole you call your new home."

Relief spasmed through her. So she hadn't been dragged back to her world. Then alarm punched her. If they hadn't gone back, her kind were still here on the human world. They hadn't come merely to tote her home for whatever sick purposes her father had devised. They had come for something else.

What the hell was it? It couldn't be good.

The guard leaned against the wall, crossing his ankles and folding his arms. Kiera noticed little gold buckles on his boots. How absurd. Her father flaunted his wealth by dressing those in his court like this as a sign that he could step on anyone he pleased. As he and his court feasted and drunk, wearing all manner of finery, peasants starved in their fields.

The assassin's guild had been cobbled together. The place had been dry and they'd had enough to eat, but any repairs came out of their paychecks. She hadn't thought about that in years or how fortunate she'd been in terms of comfort and provision since she'd come to the human world.

Those first few decades had been difficult, but then she'd met Rowan and Miles. She had not imagined that she would be taken away from them like this.

I am so stupid, Kiera thought. *Just because I was banished didn't mean I would never see him again or that he would never come for me.*

The guard was observing her like she was lunch. Kiera assumed it was the next day, but maybe more than twenty-four hours had passed since her abduction.

"Pl-please," she croaked, her pride screaming at her not to speak. "I'm thirsty."

"Of course. Where are my manners?" The mockery in his tone was unmistakable. The guard poked his head out the door and mumbled something to another guard. A few minutes later, someone came in with a waterskin. He sauntered over to Kiera and tipped it toward her mouth. What trick was this? she wondered. Maybe the water was drugged. No, they clearly wanted her awake. Maybe it wasn't water but some vile liquid.

Maybe he would bring it to her lips, then jerk it away at the last second.

"Drink up," the guard cooed.

To her surprise, the skin met her lips, and water trickled past her teeth, coating her throat. It was the best damn water she had ever tasted. He let her drink until the skin was empty, then withdrew it. It didn't seem drugged since she felt no effects.

The guard handed the skin to whoever was outside the door, then resumed his position against the wall. "You can eat later if you comply."

"With what?" she rasped. The water had helped, but her throat was still sore.

His wicked smile made her bristle. "With my questioning. I gave you water so you could speak. Don't expect the same courtesy again."

Her heart dropped. What did he want to know?

"That woman you work for is a dragon, isn't she?"

And a witch. She pushed that thought away. Some fae could not only read minds but pry into them and pluck thoughts up like picking a grape. Kiera doubted this male had that ability, but she had to be careful. "Why do you care?"

"Is she a dragon? Yes or no?"

Kiera pressed her lips together.

The fae shook his head as if disappointed. "They said you would be difficult, but I had secret hopes that you would talk to me. Very well, Princess. Have it your way. No food, and no more water. In addition, someone will whip you every morning. A healer will come in the afternoon to heal your wounds, and in the evening, whipping again."

Her father's signature torture. Kiera felt sick.

"Until you *comply*," he added.

They wanted Stacy. That was *very* bad.

I won't tell them a damn thing. I'll die first. She wanted to die out of spite, but then she would seem weak to her father.

The guard sauntered toward her with malice in his eyes. "Right now…" He touched the chain around her left wrist. Magic must have fused it together since it opened at his touch. Kiera's hand fell limply to her side. She cried out in surprise and at the sensation of blood flowing through the limb again. The guard did the same to the chain on her right wrist, and she pitched forward. Her limbs were too numb for her to soften her fall.

Pain jolted through her. As she lay there, the guard undid the chains on her ankles. Kiera knew he would have to haul her up and carry her wherever he intended to take her. She could not walk.

"Right now," he murmured again.

A jolt went through her before he said the next words.

The guard grinned. "Time to see Daddy."

CHAPTER EIGHT

Stacy finally left the office. After a long day of organizing a calendar, planning a trip to her father's estate in Pennsylvania, and taking calls from various members of the community, she needed to reconnect with her friends.

She walked toward the house through the frosty garden. The windows glowed warmly, and she pulled her cardigan around her to fend off the chill. Inside, it was quiet. Amy had gone to bed early since she was tired from her trip. Stacy assumed Ethan was in the library where he often was in the evening.

Stacy went in search of Rowan, looking first in his study. As she expected, she found him there. Stacy had offered him a larger room multiple times, but Rowan kept this space since it was where he had worked when Catherine lived here.

The dryad was worried. "Go look for her," she ordered. "Take Miles with you."

Rowan nodded.

"You might want to reach out to the Graytails. No one is better at tracking than they are."

Rowan considered that, then nodded again. "I'll call their emissary before we leave. Have you seen Miles?"

"I haven't, but he should be around." Stacy had been concerned about Kiera's well-being until she saw the pain on Rowan's face. He hurried out of the room in search of Miles while dialing the Graytails' contact. Kiera was more than capable of defending herself, so something serious must have happened.

After Rowan and Miles left, Stacy wandered down to the library. Ethan sat on the rug before the fire, legs crossed, poring over old books. The large leather volume in his lap was worn at the edges. His brows were drawn as he scrutinized the tight writing. He turned the page gingerly as if afraid it would crumble beneath his touch. He was so engrossed in his reading that he did not notice Stacy was there until she sat beside him.

He was probably looking for more information on Malabbra. Stacy was about to ask him, but then he glanced at her face and saw the worry on her features. "Stacy, what's wrong?"

"I'm worried about Kiera. Rowan and Miles left to look for her."

Ethan put an arm around her. "Then Kiera is in good hands or is about to be. Did they call the Graytails?"

Stacy nodded. "And Rowan will call us if they need backup."

She watched the flames dance. Flecks of gold swam in her eyes. "Stacy? Is there something else?"

She snapped out of her daze and stood, sighing. "It's been too long since I last flew." She smiled. "I need to blow off steam. I will be back in about an hour."

Stacy went outside, slipped into dragon form, and surged toward the dark sky.

They'd been looking for hours, but they'd found nothing. Rowan was increasingly impatient and also fighting panic and fear.

Snow fell on the four people standing at the side of the road.

They could only see the surrounding trees by the light of the moon, which had been full several days ago.

Rowan, Miles, and the two Graytails wolves had gone into the city, starting with the area Kiera had gone to first. Since it had been over a day since she was there, the wolves found it difficult to pick up her scent. They'd trailed it to an alley and found blood, but not Kiera's. She had cleaned up the mess before disappearing. The wolves noticed more than one pair of bootprints in the mud by one of the walls—Kiera's and another's. They concluded that with no signs of a struggle, Kiera had not been taken here.

They trailed her scent back to the country and reached a dead end. Rowan's mind was churning. Miles was grim as the werewolves searched the trees at the side of the road.

Rowan couldn't begin to express his gratitude to them. Without them, he and Miles would have been lost. The werewolves worked tirelessly, assuring Rowan that this was good for them. With the moon being nearly full, their instinct was to be out burning off excess energy. This search was a productive way of doing that.

Kiera had masked her scent to avoid pursuit, yet someone had found her.

Miles was murmuring something that Rowan didn't hear when one of the werewolves whistled and beckoned for them to come over. Rowan and Miles stomped through the trees, crouched where the wolf pointed, and saw Kiera's unsheathed dagger, the hilt encrusted with emeralds, gleaming on the ground. Rowan had given it to her long ago.

His heart ached at the sight. Why was it here? Kiera wouldn't have dropped her dagger, so someone had thrown it here. He scanned every trunk, branch, and curve of the path that led through Stacy's land into the Graytails' territory and past it to Victor Corbinelli's old estate.

"Rowan," Miles called. "Look at this."

Rowan saw that his friend had gone back to the road. He joined him as Miles swept a finger over the asphalt. "See there?"

Tire marks. "They could have been made after she passed."

Miles nodded. "I know, but what if this was Kiera? It looks like she was trying to avoid something or got surprised and swerved."

"Or was forced off the road," one of the wolves rumbled.

Rowan whipped his head to the male. "Can you still smell her?"

"Yes, and I smell someone else."

"Several others," the other wolf chimed in. "Their scents intermingle."

Kiera had been taken. Rowan had guessed that an hour ago, but the confirmation was like a punch to the gut. Who had abducted her? The wolves showed him the footprints—four sets other than Kiera's. She'd taken down that many with ease, so those who'd attacked her had been highly skilled and had the advantage of surprise.

"See here?" the werewolf growled. "Bootmarks, and it looks like someone, or some*thing*, was dragged."

Probably Kiera. Rowan's heart raced.

The night was long and arduous. Rowan and Miles followed the Graytails across Stacy's land and through a large portion of the Graytails.' They reached a hillside, and Rowan spied the remains of Victor's once-great estate with its werewolf camp.

"Sickening what he did here," one of the werewolves muttered.

Rowan considered the area. Stacy had burned Victor to a crisp and set his land aflame. She had wanted to buy it and grant it to the Graytails but had been locked in various legal battles with Victor's heirs for months. They crossed a stream in the forest and descended into a valley. The wolves were still moving fast, but Rowan and Miles were tired.

Would this ever be over? Rowan wondered. Would they find her?

"Keep your head up," Miles instructed him. "We will find her if it is the last thing we do." Miles was seldom this grim. His concern for Kiera, who was like a sister to him, was clear. Rowan squeezed his friend's shoulder to thank him for the encouragement. They crunched over the day-old snow. Rowan did not care that the wind was bitterly cold. Walking kept him warm.

Finally, he spotted something he had never seen before: the towers of a building he had not known was there. The werewolves were leading them in that direction.

<u>Spain, 1713</u>

Rowan was worn from battle, and dirt, sweat, tears, and the blood of those he had killed covered his clothes. He wasn't thinking about how he looked or smelled, though. He was thinking about her.

He hurried down the narrow corridor beneath flickering torchlight and reached a wooden door. He knocked, but no answer came from the other side. She might not be here. He knocked again, hoping a servant was, but there was no answer. He slowly opened the door to find a wide, open room with a bed of straw covered in wool on one wall. A closed trunk stood beside it. In an adjoining room, Rowan heard the soft splashing of water.

He did not register what was happening until he crossed the room and saw her sitting in a tub with steam wisping around her. The water rose past her breasts and was murky from the herbs she'd added to it, so all he saw were her collarbones to the top of her head.

Her wet dark hair pooled around her shoulders as she cupped the water and brought it to her face. Dirt and blood still flecked her neck and shoulders. She'd just washed the detritus of the battle from her face.

Rowan had not realized he was staring at her while she was bathing until she brought her hands away from her face. "I know you're there." She met his gaze.

Rowan started. "I-I'm... Apologies. I didn't mean..."

She laughed. "You have seen me naked before. Come in."

"Not like this," he muttered. He'd seen her naked when she'd been wounded nearly unto death on the battlefield. A healer had stripped off her clothing to get to her wounds. Rowan had not thought about her body beyond his great need to see it repaired so she would live. This... this was different.

Rowan's heart pounded, and his cheeks turned pink.

"I need your help," she murmured as if to encourage him to come closer.

Rowan knelt beside the tub, savoring the warmth rising from the water. It was tempting to get, though it could not hold the both of them. Kiera turned to reveal a gash on her shoulder blade. "I cannot reach this. Will you put my herbs on it?" She handed him a small bowl of herbs ground to a paste. Rowan took it and swept his fingers through the substance before gingerly applying it to her wound. She winced but said nothing.

As he worked, her breathing evened out, and finally, she let out a satisfied sigh. "It feels better already."

"Why do you not have a servant in here to help you?" Rowan asked.

"I wanted to be alone," was her quiet response.

"You are not alone now."

"You don't make me feel intruded upon."

Rowan's cheeks heated further. *It's the steam*, he told himself.

"Why did you come?" she asked, leaning back.

He remembered how disheveled and dirty he was and how bad he smelled. Kiera must have noticed, but she was used to the scents of the battlefield. Sweat and blood did not bother her.

He watched as she swept her fingernails along a bar of soap and dug out the dirt the soap did not reach. "I-I got you something," he stuttered.

She scanned his face.

"For your birthday," he added.

She laughed. He loved hearing that. Kiera seldom laughed. "My birthday isn't until the next full moon."

Rowan pulled a stool over and sat so they were the same height. "I know that. I was going to wait, but today..." He swallowed. *"I thought I was going to lose you."*

When he'd realized she was no longer fighting at his side, he'd almost panicked. She was here now, though. Safe, getting clean. *Which I need to do,* he reminded himself.

Kiera's face softened. *"You didn't lose me, Rowan."*

"I don't want to wait anymore." He pulled the gift off his belt. He'd had the dagger made for her. It would perfectly fit her hand, and its hilt was encrusted with emeralds. Kiera's eyes glowed as he held it up.

"Rowan..."

"Take it, Kiera. Don't say it's too much."

She hesitated. "It's perfect."

"It's enchanted, too."

She raised a brow. "Of course it is. Rowan, I have to tell you how I feel."

Rowan met her eyes and saw the same yearning he'd felt since the day he first saw her. "Kiera..." he started.

She surged up and pressed her lips to his in a tentative kiss. It took everything Rowan had not to turn it into a wild, hungry one. Kiera pulled away. "I didn't tell you, but you understand what I mean."

Rowan's jaw dropped. Maybe he should give her enchanted weapons more often. Kiera nodded at the water. "Do you want to come in?"

"There's not enough room."

Kiera smiled. "We will make room."

"Fucking hell," Miles muttered. "It's a *castle.*"

From a distance, they'd been able to tell it was a large edifice built of stone. A fortress, perhaps. The large and seemingly abandoned estate was dominated by the structure. They saw no lights or signs of life, but the scents had brought the wolves here. Both

Graytails were convinced that Kiera had been brought to this place.

Clouds filled the sky, so the moon did not provide much light. Rowan's heart thundered. What was this place? It occurred to him then that they could see it only because they had magic. To a human, this forest would look empty.

He wondered how long the castle had been here. He did not sense wards or other magical protections. If not for the scents the wolves had tracked here, he wouldn't have found it.

Rowan wanted to go in and rescue Kiera. Miles could dig tunnels with his magic and lead them within, as they had done when dealing with the vampires, but it was too big a risk, and they didn't know enough. The pain of the realization was nearly unbearable. Miles and the wolves thought the same. "We need to go back for the others," Miles offered. "Stacy and the coven will help us."

"So will we," one of the Graytails said. "I'm sure our Alpha will spare a few of us to aid you."

Rowan could not take his eyes off the building. He counted the windows and doors and mapped the paths around it. He noted where stones were loose and where the ground had been trodden down. It did not seem well guarded, but maybe it was on the inside. If they had bothered to take Kiera, they would guard her, right?

Rowan did not want to think of what might be happening to her now.

Stay strong for me, he thought as Miles tugged him away.

Miles murmured, "Let's go, Rowan. We will come back for her."

CHAPTER NINE

Stacy watched Ethan before she allowed her presence to be known. The flight had done her good, and though worry for Kiera still lodged within her, she felt better.

Ethan paced in front of the hearth, brow furrowed as he studied the pages of a worn tome. When he wasn't handling coven matters, he was here, searching for information on the dark world of Malabbra.

Stacy could have watched him for hours. His contemplative expression and the gingerly movements of his fingers on the old books brought her comfort. He was as much himself with her as he was alone, and watching him from the library's shadowed entrance reminded her of that.

Finally, Stacy stepped into the room. Ethan glanced at her, a small smile touching his lips. "I was wondering when you were going to come in instead of watching me from the doorway."

An easy smile graced her lips. His voice made her relax. "It's late, Ethan."

"I know." He motioned for her to come forward and sat on one of the sofas by the fireplace. She took a seat beside him. "I finally found something about Malabbra. This old tome was deep inside a trunk in your mother's secret room." He gestured toward the closed-off part of the library that Stacy and Rowan had discovered during her first few weeks here. The room was full of maps and old books preserved by magic. Stacy hadn't explored the whole room, but apparently, Ethan had.

He laid the open book on her lap, and the flickering firelight made shadows dance over the yellowed, wrinkled pages. The writing had faded, but Stacy still made out a series of runes etched into the paper with descriptions written in flowing script beneath. It was not a language she knew, but Ethan could tell her what it meant.

"These look familiar," Stacy murmured, fingertips tracing one of the larger runes. It took up nearly the entire page, with script in the remaining space. As she did that, a warm surge of magic traveled from the tip of the finger tracing the rune up through her arm.

"I hoped they would," Ethan replied. "This is a book of runes from many different worlds, and this section is about runes from Malabbra. Many were used in dark magic and have since been outlawed. I haven't seen or heard of anyone using runes like these in centuries. They confirm that dragons came from Malabbra like vampires and other creatures did."

Creatures like demons and warlocks. Nothing good, Stacy recalled. What did this mean for dragons as a whole and for her? Ethan continued, "I remember seeing protective dragon runes around the estate that Rowan said your father put here after your parents married."

Stacy nodded. "I've seen similar runes in my father's other houses, but they aren't the same as these." She gestured at the tome.

"They are all draconic runes," Ethan pointed out. He showed her similar curves in the runes, hard and precise. "These were the first draconic runes, as far as anyone can tell. They were on an ancient drawing of a gate into Malabbra." He turned the page, and the next drawing sprawled out, the ink reaching the edges of the page and threatening to spill over as if this small space wasn't enough to convey what it wanted.

The gate was deformed, a monster in its own right made of warty branches, shadows, and iron. Shadows swirled around and beyond it. A dark, overcast sky stretched above it, with forks of lightning cutting through the black. The gate bore the runes from the previous page, and as Stacy traced the drawing, she felt another jolt of magic. This wasn't the warm, promising magic she'd felt since learning about her heritage. This magic felt like a dagger of ice probing her veins. She jerked her finger away.

Ethan's brows furrowed. "It's affecting you, isn't it?"

Stacy nodded, turning her eyes away from the page and meeting his at last. "Everything from Malabbra is monstrous. Does that mean dragons are monsters by nature?" *Am I a monster?*

Ethan carefully closed the book and set it aside, then placed his hand over Stacy's as if he'd heard the second question too. "Maybe they were once, but it is clear that dragons left Malabbra long before any other creatures. It is possible that dragons were, and after they left the dark world, they evolved into what they—*you*—are today. We will never know. I've looked hard, but I believe only those who were there long ago could tell us."

"I could ask my father," Stacy suggested, though she doubted that Khan would know much more. Khan was proud and stubborn, but he liked sharing their history. He would have told her this too if he'd known, or so Stacy hoped.

She considered the matter. No species was considered fully good or fully bad, but it alarmed Stacy to think that dragons had come from a world of dark magic. A whole fucking world of it, a place very different from the human world. She wondered if there were good vampires or other beings on Malabbra who did not practice dark magic. She remembered people who had warned her to be cautious of the dragon magic in her veins, saying it could turn her wicked if she gave into temptation.

Stacy didn't know what to make of this except that the same could be said of any person. However, someone with magic could have a devastating effect on others if they chose temptation.

Ethan's voice interrupted her thoughts. "As far as I can tell, the dark world of Malabbra was sealed off, and the creatures there are unable to slip through the veil. I don't know what happened, but the books I've read indicate there was a war between worlds fought by creatures of many species, and in the end, the dark creatures of Malabbra were banished to their world and sealed away."

"That doesn't mean that every creature was rounded up or that they didn't go to other worlds," Stacy pointed out. Otherwise, how could there be vampires here?

Ethan squeezed her knee. "You're right, and if those monsters come at us, they won't know what hit them."

Stacy gave him an appreciative smile, then glanced at the clock on the mantle. It was past midnight. "We should go to bed." *And hope Kiera comes back with Rowan and Miles.*

At dawn, there was no word from Rowan or Miles, and neither had returned. Stacy paced around the kitchen with a cup of coffee in hand, anxiety bubbling. "I can't sit around all day wondering where they are and what they're doing," she told Ethan. "Amy and I will go visit my father's estate in Pennsylvania. We can come back quickly if we're needed."

She explained that the estate was in the state's northeastern corner in the Appalachian Mountains, near Elk Hill. Khan's parcel was spacious enough for a dragon to come and go without being seen by anyone. Stacy wasn't certain if she would find the place empty or managed by the spirits who dwelled in the land, similar to the Guardians who inhabited her estate and had since before her mother had lived here. "It's a three hour drive, but I imagine it will be much quicker using the other method." Stacy smiled knowingly.

Ethan nodded. "Go for it. I'll contact you when I hear anything from or see the others."

Amy wandered into the kitchen a moment later, wearing pajamas, her hair mussed from sleep. She frowned at Stacy as her friend handed her a cup of coffee, saying, "Drink up. You'll need your stamina for today's mission."

Ethan rose from the table, shooting Amy a grin. "Good luck."

"What did that mean?" Amy asked after Ethan left the room.

An hour later, the two women left Thorn Manor and took a narrow path leading into the forest beyond the stone wall surrounding the main grounds. Out here, Stacy had more than enough room to shift.

"Rowan is going to be mad when he finds out we went somewhere without him driving," Amy remarked.

Stacy's knowing smile returned, and flecks of gold joined the green in her eyes. "Well, then it's a good thing we aren't driving, isn't it?"

Amy looked nervous, but she mumbled, "Good thing I bundled up. This is going to be a chilly ride."

It was unlike anything she had ever imagined, starting with the temperature.

Amy had expected riding on a dragon's back to be bitterly cold at this time of year, but the clothes Stacy had loaned her were enchanted to keep her warm. The wind touched only her face, and even that was buffered by Stacy's massive body.

Amy was strapped on for safety, and although she did not have a saddle, there was a wool blanket between her and Stacy's hard scales. Stacy flew not far above the trees, knowing any human who deigned to peer up would not see her as a dragon but an odd cloud. It helped that it was overcast.

Stacy flew at a comfortable pace for Amy, careful not to dip or swoop fast. When she did, Amy's belly did somersaults. This would take some getting used to. The ground was near enough for her to make out leaves, winding paths, and frozen streams. Finally, Amy saw mountains.

Stacy rose higher. The sun peeked through the heavy clouds and illuminated the snow-dusted trees below. The roads below were empty except for the occasional car winding through the mountains. Amy thought, *I could get used to this*. She wondered what this would be like in summer when the warm wind brushed her face.

Finally, among the mountains, Amy saw a wide lake and a large house beyond. Trees surrounded the valley between two mountains. She understood why Khan had bought this land. She spotted a perfect area for a dragon to land and shift into human form. It was a shame this land hadn't been occupied for decades. It was time to change that, and Stacy had asked her to come to help her think of what to do with it.

Stacy angled her body to land, and the ground surged closer. Amy clutched the straps.

"That wasn't bad, was it?" Stacy asked after she resumed human form. She brushed snow off her pants, eyeing Amy.

Amy's eyes shone. "The landing was a bit rough, but before that…" She shook her head. "I can't believe my best friend is a dragon."

Stacy slung an arm across Amy's shoulders, laughing. "I still don't believe it sometimes." Stacy had landed beside the lake, which was partially frozen. Banks of snow on one side of the lake led to the old stone home. The house was smaller than the one on

Khan's estate in New York but bigger than the average family home.

"He calls this his fishing house," Stacy told Amy with a rueful expression. "My father once had many outdoor activities, not only flying. It doesn't look like this place has been used in years." The windows were dirty, for one thing.

"How many acres does he own?" Amy asked as she lowered her hood and pushed her braid behind her back. Her cheeks were red from the cold and wind.

"Almost a hundred," Stacy replied. "Most of it is forest, so no one can come close to the valley and see...well, what I just did."

"A dragon transforming into a person. Pretty alarming if you've never seen it before," Amy mused.

Stacy smiled, removed her arm from around Amy's shoulders, then strode toward the house to get a closer look. Before they had gone far, Amy murmured, "Look, someone is coming. So much for no one being able to get close."

The man had shoulder-length blond hair and a trimmed beard. He wore a thick winter coat, jeans, and boots, and a puzzled expression. He seemed to think they were intruding, which meant...

He manages this place for my father, Stacy thought. She was about to smile and introduce herself when the man aimed a rifle at them.

"Whoa!" Amy put up her hands. "Hello to you, too."

Stacy also put up her hands as the man demanded, "Who are you, and what are you doing here?"

"Are you the caretaker?" Stacy asked.

"You're not supposed to be here," he responded coldly. "No one is."

"You're talking to Stacy Drakethorn," Amy snapped. "Her father owns this land. Who the hell are *you*, and why are you here?"

The man lowered the rifle. "Are you really? I'm sorry if that's true. It's only that no one has come here for ten years, much less anyone who knows Khan. You're his daughter?" He glanced behind her at the patch of snow disturbed by her dragon form. That was evidence enough.

Stacy nodded. "You must be Elliot."

He nodded. Amy glanced at Stacy. "You know who he is?"

"Yesterday, Reginald found records that listed the estate managers my father employs. Elliot Woodsen manages this property. I'm surprised you're still here." *Was* he managing the place? Maybe when things were growing, he maintained the grounds. He certainly didn't maintain the house. "You were employed about fifty years ago."

Elliot nodded again.

"But you're, like, thirty!" Amy exclaimed, then realized he must be paranormal like Stacy. "What are you?"

Elliot chuckled and glanced at Stacy. "I take it your father didn't list what I am in the records."

"No, only your name and the year you came to work here." Stacy gestured at the house. "Do you live there?"

Elliot shook his head and balanced the rifle on his shoulder. He came closer, and the women made out his features. He had brown eyes and a few scars flecking his face. He was broad-shouldered and muscular. Stacy thought he looked like a lumberjack. He had an easy, relaxed way about him now that he knew they were not a threat—or not a threat to him.

"I live near here with my pack and come by every so often to check on things. Make sure no one is intruding and all that. I didn't think I would find anyone here, much less Constantine Drakethorn's daughter." He tilted his head, and his hair fell over his face. He pushed it aside. "I've heard about you. You helped a pack get their land back in New York, right?"

"The Graytails," Stacy confirmed, remembering that though werewolf packs were often rivals, they united against a common enemy. News traveled quickly, especially to nearby packs. She wasn't surprised that the news of the Graytails' win had spread. "You're a werewolf too?"

Elliot nodded. "My pack is small, but we have lived in these mountains for generations. I have cousins in the Graytails, and I met your father through them." Stacy found that interesting since Khan had often shown distaste for werewolves. He must have liked Elliot enough to hire him to watch over this land. The werewolf eyed Amy. "I can't determine what you are."

"A boring human," Amy chirped.

"She's an investigative journalist and a valuable member of my team," Stacy added. "We've come to check on this estate and see if I should sell or keep it. My father has an abundance of land, and he doesn't need to keep all of it."

Elliot peered at Stacy before nodding. "I can show you around if you'd like, though I don't know how to get into the house. I only handle the outside, so I imagine the building is in some disrepair."

Stacy eyed the house. They wouldn't need it, depending on what she did with the place. She smiled at Elliot. "Show us your favorite places, please."

They tromped through the snow. Not much had fallen in the valley, but Stacy was glad she'd worn boots. Amy stayed at her side while Elliot led them past the house toward a grove of trees and a path that went down the mountain. "This is the entrance. There's a garage up that way and a large shack with fishing supplies. You can go inside both of those."

"Does my father keep any vehicles here?" Stacy asked.

"Not that I know of. Not in the garage, anyway."

When they entered the Grove, Elliot lowered his voice. "The grounds here are rich with magic, and many spirits live nearby." He gestured at the trees. "Some live here. When there is a full moon, you can see some of them. Others form over the lake on those nights."

Stacy realized her father had come here when he needed to get away.

"I imagine the thick magic here helps your pack," Amy offered.

Elliot smiled. "We do benefit by living near this estate. Though we don't use this land, it helps that no one comes here. We're left in peace."

Had Khan done that intentionally? Stacy had a hard time imagining it, but her father often surprised her.

"The pack's elders say that this land has belonged to the dragon since they came here," Elliot explained. "Many years before I was born, your father saved them from an attack. Without him, I would not exist." Elliot held Stacy's gaze, resolve in his eyes.

A smile tugged at her lips. "My father surprises me sometimes. I am glad he did that for your people."

"Having heard what you did for my cousins and their pack," Elliot went on, "it makes sense that you are his daughter."

"What else can you tell me about this place? How often did my father come here?"

"Not often," Elliot amended. "The last time I saw him was over two decades ago. Almost twenty-five years, I think."

Stacy and Amy shared a glance. The timeline matched. Khan had come here after Catherine's death to be alone and mourn. Stacy's heart ached at the thought of her father wandering this land under the full moon, meeting the mountains' spirits and wishing he could bring his wife back.

"Did a woman ever come with him?" Stacy asked.

"Your mother?" Elliot shook his head. "Not that I know of, though Khan came here sometimes when I wasn't around, so it is possible."

Amy tapped her chin, a sign that an idea was forming in her mind. She didn't articulate it, though. Stacy was about to ask Elliot another question when her phone buzzed in her back pocket—a text from Ethan. She murmured to Amy, "Rowan and Miles are back with news, but Kiera isn't with them." Instant worry took over her features. "Thank you for showing us this place, Elliot, but we must go. I'll be in touch, and I will be back when I have matters at home cleared up."

Elliot gave them a curt nod. "Come anytime. If I am not here, I will be nearby and know you have come onto the grounds. The wards tell me." So that was how he'd known she was here.

Stacy and Amy headed toward the lake, and Elliot went in the opposite direction. Stacy was glad for that since although she felt she could trust the werewolf, she didn't want him seeing her shift. "What plan are you cooking up in that head of yours?" she asked Amy as they approached the lake.

"We have other things to worry about right now," Amy hedged.

"I still want to hear your idea."

"Well, I'm still forming it, but I was thinking a secluded place like this so rich in magic might make a perfect place for a school."

Stacy halted, raising a brow.

"Young witches or other magicals could come here to learn or practice what they know without the fear of being seen or interrupted by non-magicals. It would also prevent others from knowing where you live if they come here instead of to our home."

Stacy smiled. "This is why I need you, Amy. You have the best ideas. I will consider it further. Right now, we need to get home."

CHAPTER TEN

The rough tug of chains was a minor pain compared to the dread Kiera felt as the fae guards led her from her dungeon up a long, winding stone staircase to the main level where her father, the king of the fae, awaited.

The dungeons were a labyrinth of narrow corridors and square cells, most with the doors open and pungent odors oozing out into the passages. As far as Kiera could tell, there were no other prisoners held here, or not in cells. The guards and any other fae who did as the king bade them were prisoners too, even if they did not wear the heavy chains Kiera was burdened with.

They passed so many cells in so many corridors that Kiera lost count despite her efforts to memorize a way out. She had the sense that they'd led her in circles to confuse her. It didn't help that her head was still throbbing and her body screamed in pain. The last time she saw her father, he had tortured her to within an inch of her life, then banished her to the human world.

Kiera knew he would torture her again. This would not be the painful whippings he'd given her before but something deeper and psychological. There would be no banishing, though. This was not his world, and he had nowhere to send her to but her death.

Kiera wished he would kill her. It would be a mercy.

The stone staircase was torturous in its own right. It wound up and up for an eternity. Kiera could hardly stand, let alone walk or climb, but when she slowed, the guard ahead of her jerked on her chain while the guard behind her jammed the hilt of his sheathed sword into her back. Kiera was sweating, humiliated, and on the brink of collapse when they reached the top of the stairs.

They halted for a moment, and Kiera heaved in icy air. This castle was old and drafty, but that wasn't the only source of coldness. It was the presence of her father and king, formerly the sole ruler of her small, pitiful life. They were standing in a wide hall, and Kiera spied arched wooden doors banded in iron that presumably led outside. Not that it mattered since she couldn't escape now.

"This way," one of the guards growled, tugging her toward another set of doors as if she were a disobedient dog on a leash. They thought she was if the many times they had called her a bitch was any indication.

These doors opened into a large, rectangular throne room. Perhaps he'd redecorated the drafty medieval room to his liking. She wondered how long this place had been here and how her father had known of it. Maybe this was a secret place in the human world he used as a touchstone.

Kiera's cut and blistered feet hurt as they pulled her toward the room. Despite her dread, Kiera was relieved by the sunlight pouring through the windows. She wanted to feel the warmth of the sun one last time before her father made the rest of her life hell.

The guard yanked her into the room, then halted. Kiera nearly smacked into the back of the lead guard. "Watch it," the guard behind her snarled. Kiera straightened, rolling her shoulders back. The stone throne on the dais was empty, as the room seemed to be at first.

Kiera knew her father hadn't changed. She had hardly a moment to twist her head and locate him before the guard in back of her shoved her to her knees and growled, "You will bow before your king." Kiera winced when his saliva hit her skin, then groaned at the pain wincing brought to her swollen eye. She could partially open it now.

Finally, *he* appeared. Kiera's heart lurched into her throat.

The fae king materialized before her. She had learned that from him and used the skill throughout her time in the human realm. It had served her well, but she hated that he could do it.

Kiera hadn't seen her father in centuries, but he looked exactly as he had when he'd sent her away. His silver hair fell down his back like a waterfall in contrast to the dark inkiness of his eyes. His skin was a luminous white. Kiera's had formerly looked like that, but years in the human world had changed her. It now had texture and was darkened by the sun, not to mention the bruises, swelling, and cuts caused by the guards' attentions that her fae magic had not been able to heal.

She was far from the princess she'd once been, lacking a sumptuous robe and a crown. She preferred the chains since they were obvious signs of her captivity.

Her father's name was Alerion Thraxius, and he was the sole fae king anyone remembered. Kiera had tried to find out if that was true, but most books in his realm were accessible only with his permission. Another secret. He had many.

A cruel smile split his lips, and she heard the voice from her worst nightmares. "Hello, Adrilonziglia."

She had fought hard to forget that name. She had formerly been Adrilonziglia Thraxius or Lia. Kiera uttered the same words she'd spoken to the fae seer Cyprian months ago. "That is not my name anymore."

Alerion laughed as if she were a child making a joke she did not understand. "That's right. You go by a senseless human name now. Kiera Swiftshadow, isn't it? Your reputation precedes you."

How had he discovered her new name, let alone her reputation?

Alerion saw the question on her face, and his smile widened. He kept his hands behind his back, and the shimmering of his golden robe was almost blinding in the sunlight. Kiera gauged that it was morning. "That sniveling traitor Cyprian gave you away, daughter dear. He found you in this world and came to me, relating your exploits and maneuverings. He hoped the information would buy him a place in my court."

The king paused, and the glint in his eyes told Kiera what had happened before he said it. "I severed his head from his neck and watched it roll along the floor. Many try to please me, and most fail."

A warning that he could do the same to her. He wouldn't, though. If Alerion had wanted to kill his daughter, he would have done it centuries ago. She wasn't sad to hear that Cyprian was dead since he'd sold her out.

The fae king tilted his head, examining her. "You have changed, daughter."

No shit. "You haven't," she snarled.

The king shook his head as if disappointed. "You are wrong, Lia."

She bristled at her former nickname but saw no point in correcting him. She was still on her knees, and the stone floor was far from comfortable. The shackles on her wrists chafed as the guard holding them shifted. Alerion's eyes flicked to the guard. "Let her go. My daughter and I must catch up." It was strange hearing her father use a human phrase.

The guard obeyed; he did not unlock her chains, but he did let them clatter to the floor. The sound made Kiera wince. The guards stepped back toward the door. "Rise, Lia," Alerion commanded.

She considered staying on her knees to spite him, but she stood slowly, wobbling as she rose. The chains clinked, adding to the pulsing headache she'd borne since she'd opened her eyes. Alerion gestured at a table nearly as long as the room that was laden with an array of food.

Kiera's mouth watered, and her stomach rumbled. The banquet included roasted venison seasoned to perfection, many salads, and fruit and nuts. There was bread with honey and pitchers of wine. Kiera had learned to cook in the assassin's guild and used that skill in the human world.

Kiera tore her eyes away from the food and opened her mouth to retort, but Alerion cut her off. "Spare me the dramatics. Take a seat. Eat if you want, or don't touch it. I don't care. We're going to talk either way."

Well, *he* would talk. "What do you want?" she demanded.

Alerion sighed. "I forgot how insolent you are. You inherited that from your whore mother."

Kiera stiffened. Her mother had become pregnant with Kiera when Alerion had spied her serving food and decided his day would be better if he raped her. Alerion had many bastards, including daughters, and he set them to work in fields or to beg for their keep in his villages. When she was born, an oracle had named Kiera one of his most powerful children, so he'd kept her. Kiera had often wished she had been thrown out then.

She saw no use in defending her sidhe mother, who had died long ago. Alerion probably didn't remember her name or what she looked like, and Kiera looked fae.

"I want your help, daughter," the king stated at last. Kiera hadn't known that the word "help" was included in her father's vocabulary. "Let that sink in. This is the only time I will ever say that to you."

This had to be a trick. He had many up his golden sleeves.

Alerion glided to the head of the long table and took his seat, but Kiera remained standing. She thought of a dozen ways to take him out, but none would work. She didn't have a chance, given the guards at the door and in her weakened state. Even if she was at full strength and the guards were gone, Alerion was the most powerful fae. She might challenge him, but he would defeat her in the end.

Alerion poured himself a cup of wine and watched her over the rim as he drank. After he set it down, he spoke again. "Tell me everything you know about Anastasia Drakethorn and her father."

Kiera bristled. No way in hell would she tell him *anything*.

Alerion was no longer smiling. If she didn't speak, the remainder of her life would be spent in the cell. Alerion sighed when she did not respond. "I thought it would be this way. You were foolish to fall for humans."

"*You* sent me here," Kiera bit out.

"So I did. I did not realize it would make you weak."

Maybe it *was* weak that she had learned to love others. Maybe it *was* weak that she had people to fight for instead of only her selfish purposes. If that was weakness, she was proud of it, but Kiera did not think it was. Her father was blinded by greed and ambition. Perhaps he had never known how to love. He'd never loved her, though he thought he did in his own twisted way.

"You have wasted your time consorting with humans and dragons," Alerion continued. He sat back and laughed. "Look at you, smaller and weaker than ever. Pitiful."

She heard "coward," "failure," and "unwanted" in her mind, words he had hurled at her since she was young. Kiera thought about her mother and the sidhe kin she had never met and probably never would. That made her heart ache.

"What do you want with Stacy?" she demanded.

Alerion raised a brow. "You call her by a different name."

When Kiera did not respond, he sighed. "The truth is, our world is not what it used to be. It is falling apart."

Kiera had not cared about her homeworld since she'd left, but her breath caught in her throat. "What do you mean, it's falling apart?"

Alerion's expression shifted, but Kiera could not name the emotions on his face. "We depleted the magic in the land and cannot bring it back. The trees have died, the grass is stiff and brown, and the rivers are drying up one by one."

"What of the people?" Kiera asked, her voice tight.

"We are fine."

"I meant the people outside your damn court!" Her voice shook.

Alerion frowned as if confused. "They died in the famine."

Kiera felt sick. Anger bubbled within her, but she could not get her magic to react. The chains around her wrists prevented that. She realized why her father was here. "You came to the human world because it is still rich in magic. You want to take it over."

Alerion nodded, unsmiling. He took no pleasure in having to move into another world, though Kiera was certain he'd find joy in killing whoever he had to to get what he wanted. She could imagine the mass slaughter. The humans would die, and probably magicals, all so he and his court could continue living as they had. If she'd had food in her stomach, she would have hurled it.

"We seek the magic running through this world," Alerion said as if reciting a poem he'd written long ago. "Starting with the very roots. There is much in this world I despise, but I will do away with it. The human cities are hideous. I will wipe them off the face of the land and replace them with the great houses we built on our world." He made it sound like it wouldn't take centuries to accomplish. To him, that didn't seem like much. He'd lived almost a millennium.

What did this have to do with Stacy?

It was as though Alerion had read her thought. Maybe he had. "The Drakethorns have long stood in our way, so I must remove them before we begin our quest. With them opposing us, we cannot hope for victory."

Kiera was proud of her friend. Stacy was threatening enough for Alerion, king of the fae, to consider her an obstacle, and he was right. Many had underestimated Stacy, including Victor, Hines, Voss, and the other vampires. Alerion was not stupid, however. He would not underestimate a woman with dragon power.

"What do you mean the Drakethorns have long stood in your way?" Kiera asked. She wanted to stall, but she was genuinely curious.

Alerion tapped the arm of his chair, his expression thoughtful. "I have not shared much of our history with you, Lia, and I will not do so now since you have yet to tell me what you know about *her*."

Something occurred to Kiera as he said this. "You found a way into this world without being caught. Someone let you in, or at the very least, they helped you. Who the fuck was it?"

There was that cruel smile. "I would tell you, but as I said, you have yet to answer my question."

Someone with power and influence who operated from the shadows. Kiera's heart beat faster. Had this person helped the fae watch her for weeks, too? They'd known her route home and intercepted her.

Kiera's eyes widened. "Fucking hell. They used me as bait to get you to come here, didn't they?"

Cyprian might have had a hand, but Kiera didn't think the old fae seer had worked alone. Not that it mattered since he was dead. She had to escape, get to Stacy, and warn her.

Alerion insisted, "Tell me what you know."

Kiera bared her teeth. "You can plunder my mind, can't you? I won't tell you shit."

Alerion sighed once more. "I wanted to give you a chance to tell me yourself." He waved a hand at one of the guards. "Take her back to the cell. I will give her the rest of the night to comply." He gazed at her as if he were boring into her mind. "If she chooses not to, I will take what I desire."

Kiera didn't bother protesting as the guard yanked on her chains and led her back to the dungeon.

CHAPTER ELEVEN

There were five men in the library, but Stacy's eyes went to Rowan. She'd seen him grim-faced and concerned, but not like this. His hair was awry, and his skin was chapped from the cold wind. His clothes were rumpled, dirty, and torn. Miles looked the same, but that was his normal appearance. Miles' usual cheer was missing, however. He was more solemn than Stacy had ever seen him.

"What happened?" she asked.

Miles was leaning against the mantle, eyes fixed on the fire. Ethan sat on the sofa opposite him, and Rowan was hunched in a leather armchair, face buried in his hands. Stacy thought he was crying, but when he raised his head, she saw anguish on his face but no tears.

The two werewolves who'd gone with them stood near the door like sentries and nodded curtly at Stacy.

"Did you find her?" Stacy asked before anyone could answer her first question.

"We think we found where she is," Miles answered. "We came back because there was no way in hell we could get in and out without being caught. We need backup."

"Witches and wolves, if possible," Ethan requested.

Stacy dropped onto the sofa beside him while Amy went to get coffee. "Tell me everything."

Rowan didn't speak, so Miles shared what had happened, from finding Kiera's dagger in the forest near the estate to tracking her to the castle. He added, "Only magicals can see it."

Rowan raised his head, his green eyes stormy. Miles described the castle and why the werewolves thought Kiera was inside it.

"Do you have any idea who took her?" Ethan asked, worry filling his voice.

The other men shook their heads. "The wolves couldn't tell what they were by their scents," Rowan murmured.

"So they're not from here," Ethan mused.

It hit Stacy. Anyone who tried to abduct Kiera had to be as skilled as she was, and very few people did. Stacy swallowed hard. "Rowan, do you think…" Her voice trailed off, the thought too painful to put into words.

Rowan nodded curtly. "She was taken by fae."

Miles looked startled. Ethan cursed.

"I'm sorry. Did you say fucking *fae* took her?" Amy asked as she reentered the room, carrying a tray. She passed out cups.

Rowan stated, "That makes the most sense."

"That means the fae have come to our world," Miles added.

"Yes." Rowan stared into his coffee.

Ethan glanced at Stacy. "You have a plan. I can see it on your face."

She nodded. "We're going to get the backup we need and go there tonight. We will rescue Kiera and find out who the fuck is behind this."

Ethan laid a hand on her knee. "This could be a trap. It probably is. They might have taken Kiera to get to you."

"Then they'll fucking get me," Stacy snarled. When Ethan's face tightened, she added, "Sorry. I only meant that if it's a trap, I plan on walking out in human or dragon form. I don't care which."

She stood and looked at Miles and the werewolves. "Please ask the Graytails to send whatever aid they can." She addressed Ethan next. "Contact the witches in our coven. Not Claire. We haven't initiated her, so she will sit this one out."

Ethan, Miles, and the werewolves nodded and left. The silence that fell over those who remained was tense. Amy glanced at Stacy and left as well. Stacy sat at the end of the sofa by the armchair. Rowan was still staring into his coffee. Stacy couldn't imagine what was running through his head. She placed her hand on his forearm, which got his attention. His eyes met hers, and she saw tears swimming in them.

"It was awful, leaving her there," he ground out, throat tight.

"I know," Stacy murmured.

"We must go back."

"We will. Tonight, when we have the help we need." She scrutinized his face. Rowan and Kiera had been through hell and back before he'd come to the Thorn estate to work for Catherine. Once, Rowan had thought he and Kiera would never connect again. Stacy ached for the dryad. She missed Kiera too. If anything happened to the woman, Stacy would not forgive herself. *This only happened because Kiera was doing me a favor.*

"Don't do that," Rowan muttered. Stacy's eyes met his. "Don't blame yourself."

"*You're* blaming yourself," Stacy pointed out.

"I sent her out."

She gripped his arm. "Don't." It was a command.

Rowan sagged back and sighed.

"You and Miles need to rest until sundown. Then we will leave together. I know sleeping will be difficult, but try."

Rowan gave her the barest nod, and she rose and walked out of the library.

Stacy went to Amy's office upstairs. Amy was sitting behind

the desk, frowning at her PC screen. "What are you looking at?" Stacy asked as she entered.

"A map of the area Miles described. No castles from what I see. Nothing but trees, so the place *is* shielded from human eyes." Amy glanced at Stacy. "Whoever took Kiera means business. Please be careful."

"I will. Always." Stacy sat in the other chair. "I will ask Reginald to check the defenses at my father's estate, too. I want you and some wolves to stay here and defend this place while I'm gone."

Amy nodded. "On it."

Stacy smiled. "I can always count on you, Amy."

Amy stood. "Bring our girl home, okay?"

Stacy went to the armory and strapped on a belt and vest with an array of knives, most of them gifts from Kiera. It felt wrong to be arming up without Kiera at her side. For the past several months, they had dressed out and armed up side by side in silence and with precision. Without the slap of buckles and the song of knives sliding into their sheaths, it felt too quiet.

We will bring you back, Kiera. We will make those bastards who took you pay.

When Stacy heard footsteps on the stone stairs leading to the armory, Stacy turned. Rowan's face was blank, and he was peering into the distance. When he saw her, his eyes glimmered with determination. He loaded up, first with boots and vest, then with armor, weapons, and cloak. Stacy never tired of watching experienced warriors prepare for battle.

Rowan worked with a precision that spoke of years of fighting. Stacy imagined that Miles did it just as easily. *He's thinking about their past and everything he, Kiera, and Miles have been through together.* The weight of their mission hit her.

After Rowan had slung his favorite ax over his back, he asked, "Ready?"

Stacy nodded. "Are you?"

His expression was steely. "Yes."

She laid a comforting hand on his vambrace. "We will not fail. Kiera is alive, and we are going to bring her home."

Emotion flickered through his eyes. Stacy wondered if she'd said what she had for Rowan's sake or her own. She was still trying to convince herself that Kiera was not yet beyond saving. Rowan opened his mouth to reply, but Ethan appeared on the stairs with news.

"The coven and the pack are on their way. We can leave soon."

"She will be here soon," Ethan told the coven as he entered the library. Stacy and Rowan were still in the armory. Five heads turned to him.

"Tell us what's going on," one person muttered. Ethan glanced at the pair by the window, Demetrius and Diana. If not for the difference in gender, they could be the same person. The woman sat on the window sill, one leg dangling, foot nearly touching the floor. Her brother leaned against the wall beside the window, arms folded and dark eyes sweeping the room. There wasn't a detail he missed.

Everyone called them Dem and Di. Both were tall and lanky, with pale skin and black hair cut below their ears, enhancing the sharpness of their cheekbones and jaws. Although they were twins, they couldn't have been more different in personality. Demetrius was solemn and reserved, seldom speaking. His sister usually spoke for both of them.

"Stacy has a better understanding of the situation," Ethan replied mildly. "We should wait until she and Rowan join us."

Miles was still trying to get more Graytails to join them, and Ethan didn't know where Amy was.

All the coven only knew that something serious had happened, and they were eager to know more. They had yet to perform any rituals as a unit in a hostile engagement, and this mission would test them. It wasn't ideal since Kiera's life was on the line, but they needed the backup, and the coven was comprised of competent witches.

The twins, who were in their thirties, were hybrids, or as some pure-bred paranormals called them, "magical mutts." They were half-witch, half-elf, but they were not permitted to live among the elves, their father's family. As progressive as she was, Elentya had not been able to convince her people to allow that.

Orphaned as teenagers, the two had only had one another. This past summer, they'd heard about Stacy and come to her, wanting to help someone who could make the world better for people like them. Ethan remembered the day they'd reached the estate, Demetrius silently backing his sister as Diana demanded to see the mistress of the house. They were the first to be recruited into the coven, and shortly after that, they became the coven's Sentinels, tasked with protecting everyone physically and spiritually. They were adept at setting wards and using defensive magic.

Diana glowered at Ethan's response. She and Demetrius shared a look; Ethan could have sworn they were telepathic in the way of twins. A male witch spoke from beside the empty fireplace. "I am sure Ms. Drakethorn would not have called us here unless it was serious."

Ethan glanced at Emile, the oldest member of the coven. He had been friends with Ethan's grandparents and had mentored Ethan when he was a child. He had moved away when Ethan reached adulthood but had come back to the city earlier this year. After hearing that Ethan was working for a wealthy heiress with the familiar last name of Drakethorn, he'd come to the estate offering his services. He was the most knowledgeable among them by far.

He had short graying hair and a neatly trimmed beard, pleasant eyes, and he always wore jeans and a black turtleneck. When Emile came to the Thorn estate, Ethan made him the coven's Lorekeeper, tasked with maintaining the coven's traditions, knowledge, and wisdom. Ethan couldn't have imagined a better fit.

A woman sitting opposite Emile sniffed. "Anastasia is dismantling the underworld one crook at a time. Perhaps one finally proved challenging."

Ethan eyed Agatha. "No."

"Then what is it?" Diana asked.

Demetrius shot his sister a look, not a warning but a question. *"Why bother? He said he wouldn't tell us yet."*

Agatha spoke again before Ethan could, her chin raised so her graying brown hair swayed in the dying sunlight. "Anastasia must consider it very serious to call upon us. She has plenty of help without the coven."

Ethan kept his retort behind his teeth. Agatha, a seer, was nearly as old as Emile. No one would have guessed her age since she was quick, precise, blunt, capable, and powerful. She was also temperamental. Ethan sometimes wondered if she would eventually disrupt the coven's cohesiveness, but she was too valuable to lose. Agatha couldn't see the future in detail, but she picked up patterns.

It had taken Ethan and Stacy time to figure out Agatha's role in the coven, but they had finally settled on naming her the Nexus—the coven's anchor to the natural world. Agatha was attuned to the rhythms of nature and the cosmos, so she guided the coven in rituals that aligned with celestial events and natural cycles.

"It is," Ethan answered curtly. Normally, the coven members

weren't this bristly. Perhaps the anticipation of a real battle had set them on edge.

Ethan had only been in the library for three minutes by his watch, and he wished Stacy would walk through the damn door. She'd told him she would be up when she found her favorite cloak.

Ethan turned to someone standing in a corner, masked by the shadows. Like Dem, he hadn't expected Nox to speak. The woman looked to be in her late twenties, but no one knew her true age. She was Kiera's twin in terms of abilities, although she was not a fae-sidhe hybrid. Nox was proficient in protection and healing spells. Ethan did not remember her speaking since her initial interview. At least Demetrius would sometimes warn his sister not to say anything stupid.

Nox had been the last to join the coven, and a sense of peace and cohesiveness had come over the group the moment she did. Stacy had made her the coven's Harmonizer. Not only did she foster well-being between individuals, but she could heal them. Not that they had needed that ability yet.

They might tonight. They had no idea what they were walking into or what state Kiera would be in. They would probably need her abilities most tonight.

Stacy finally strode in, and all eyes snapped to her. Emile looked placid, and Agatha got nonchalant. Diana relaxed, and Demetrius' eyes went to the coven's joint Visionaries. Nox looked at Ethan and Stacy as well.

Rowan came in behind her, armored up and grim-faced.

The witches noted their apparel and weapons. "Are we going to battle?" Di asked, her smile fiendish.

Stacy swept past Ethan and stood in the center of the room, gold flecks in her eyes. He felt a swell of pride and admiration for his lover. The dragon spoke. "Not battle. One of the members of my household was taken, possibly by paranormals from another world. We need to get her back and find out what the threat is."

Stacy motioned for Rowan to stand beside her. He told the coven about Kiera's disappearance and what he, Miles, and the werewolves had discovered. At the mention of the castle and possibly that fae had taken her, the coven had a plethora of reactions.

Emile gasped. Di cursed. Demetrius' brows drew together. Nox's eyes flickered with worry. Agatha stated, "The fae wouldn't come here. Their world is far away. They wouldn't bother with us."

"And yet, they did and are," Rowan responded icily.

Agatha gazed at Stacy. "Is this truly a coven matter?"

Stacy stiffened. "It is if I say it is." She regretted the words as soon as they left her mouth. She was their leader, but she wanted them to understand her reasoning. "Kiera is a valued member of my household as well as my friend, and we will need her if this fae threat is real. This is a coven matter because if this threat is real, it will eventually affect all of us."

The witches processed her words. Finally, Diana muttered, "Then why isn't Kiera in the coven?"

Ethan shot her a look, and she diverted her gaze out the window.

"I am happy with this coven as it is," Stacy replied. "You don't *have* to help us, but I am asking you to back me."

"We will help," Demetrius agreed.

Emile nodded. "Of course."

Agatha gave a curt nod. "Wouldn't miss it."

Nox silently joined the others.

"Good," Stacy said. "We have a plan. We will—"

They all turned to the door as Miles hurried in, huffing. "Five of the Graytails agreed to help, and the sun is down. We should go."

Stacy turned to the coven. "I will tell you the plan on the way."

CHAPTER TWELVE

Moonlight dimly illuminated the light dusting of snow on the ground. The wind blew cold through the leafless trees, but Stacy's enchanted clothing kept her warm.

Surrounded by dense forest the castle Rowan and Miles had found loomed before them. Stacy observed the intimidating edifice from a safe distance. This castle was far older than any grand house on Earth, and it alarmed her that she had not been aware of its presence. Whoever was in charge must have shielded it from magicals too, like the Thorn estate was covered in illusion magic. How long had it been here, and how had the fae found it? Perhaps it had belonged to them for a long time.

Or they stole it from someone else. Ethan stood on Stacy's right, and Rowan was like a block of stone on her left. Miles and the five Graytails in wolf form were behind the dryad. Their eyes gleamed with excitement and anticipation, hackles rising when they caught the fae's scent.

The five witches stood behind Ethan. Stacy looked at each in turn, and they nodded to confirm they were as ready as they could be. She took a deep breath and nodded at Miles.

He stepped ahead of the others to work his magic. As he did,

Stacy noted that there were no wards around the building. Either the fae were fine with being infiltrated, or they did not think they would be. Either way, their pride was disconcerting.

She felt like they were walking into a trap, but it had to be done.

The ground opened under Miles' direction, and a tunnel yawned before them, long and dark. It was tall enough for Rowan to walk through without hitting his head but so narrow they had to walk single file. Miles went in first, extending the tunnel as he walked. Rowan was second, followed by Stacy, then Ethan and the coven. The werewolves brought up the rear.

The tunnel somehow felt colder than the November wind had. All Stacy heard was the group's soft breathing and the thuds of their boots on the ground. Eventually, they reached a stone wall. Miles quietly broke through, and the company entered a dank passage. The walls were stone, and the nearby cells were empty but smelled as though they had not been for long. The corridor told Stacy the castle was as old as its exterior suggested. This place was medieval. No such places had existed in America during that time, though. Or had they, shielded by magic? She had learned not to rule anything out.

The passage was empty, quiet, and even colder than the tunnel. It was not the same type of chill they'd felt outside and in the tunnel but a deeper, pervading feeling. Dark magic.

Before Stacy had time to consider that further, one of the witches cried out in alarm. Stacy spun to see guards in gold capes and armor materialize out of thin air.

Stacy's shield blazed into being, and she blocked a blade one guard slashed at her. She saw a flash of amber eyes, pointed ears, and skin smoother than silk, so the guards were fae.

So much for infiltrating quietly.

The guard quickly recovered and swung again. Stacy blocked once more, aware of the chaos in the passage. The coven witches, including Ethan, flung magic. The werewolves lunged, snarling as they leapt on the guards. Rowan drew his ax, and Miles stood near the tunnel, keeping it open so they could make a fast getaway.

Stacy was determined to rescue Kiera, no matter how many fae materialized. There were ten right now.

Kiera had been the bait. This attack confirmed that.

She and the fae guard exchanged blows until Stacy formed a fiery orb and flung it at the man. The guard screamed as the magical flames scorched his armor. Stacy lunged at a joint in his armor, and her sword sank into his side. He slumped against the wall and slid to the floor.

"This is a trap, isn't it?" she ground out, but the guard was silent in death.

As Stacy withdrew her blade, the fae's blood dripped on the floor. She had little time to consider what had happened since she was attacked from behind. The fae guard flung magic at her, and it hit her shield. It took all of Stacy's energy and focus to keep the shield intact. He lunged then, swiping his sword across it, and her shield guttered and fell. Stacy's sword hit his arm hard enough for him to drop his blade.

The guard launched another blue-green bolt of magic that sent Stacy crashing into the stone wall. He advanced toward her but only made it two steps before an ax split his back. He fell at Rowan's feet.

Stacy told her friend, "Find her." Rowan nodded, then signaled for the wolves to follow him in case he encountered trouble on the way.

The coven and the wolves had taken out most of the guards. Stacy and Ethan finished off the last two with blasts of magic. They'd been on the defense too much to keep any of the guards alive for questioning.

"They're fucking good," Ethan muttered. "I don't think we would have survived if not for our backup." He nodded at the other witches.

Stacy agreed. Centuries of war had forged these warriors, so she couldn't help being satisfied that they had taken them down so quickly. Then she thought about the possibility that these were the guards their leader could do without, so he'd thrown them at the wolves and witches. Others might await them farther down the passage since the fae had apparently known they were coming.

Stacy was sweating. The fight had drained nearly all her magic. Diana was kneeling on the floor, biting back pain. Demetrius was beside her, and Nox knelt in front of her, working her healing magic. Aside from Di, no one else seemed to be badly wounded.

"You can stay here or go back through the tunnel," Stacy told her.

Diana raised her head, dark eyes flashing in defiance. "I will come with you."

"Can you walk?" her brother asked.

Diane nodded and winced. "I will."

Stacy exchanged looks with Ethan. "If it becomes too much, Di, go back. Do you understand?"

She nodded. "I understand."

Stacy gestured down the corridor. "Let's find Rowan. I hope he hasn't run into any trouble."

The dungeon labyrinth took them longer to traverse than Stacy had expected. Rowan stood within Kiera's cell, a werewolf at his side. The other four Graytails were elsewhere, perhaps taking out nearby guards. Stacy halted when she saw Kiera suspended from chains anchored to the floor and ceiling. Her head slumped forward. She was unconscious, and she'd been badly beaten.

Stacy's heart clenched. Kiera's hair was matted with blood and sweat. Her face was marred by bruises and cuts. Her clothing was torn. When Stacy went around her, she saw that her shirt was ripped across the back, and still-bleeding whip marks glistened on her skin.

Rowan's face cycled through a dozen emotions. "Help me with her chains," he requested in a shaking voice. Stacy started at Kiera's wrists, melting the chains while being careful not to damage her skin, then did the same to the chains around her ankles. When Kiera fell, Rowan caught her.

Nox entered the cell and knelt beside Kiera to heal her. Rowan held Kiera close, tears welling in his eyes. "Come back to me," he whispered over and over. The slight movements of her chest told them she was alive.

She noted the glowing sigils on the chains that prevented Kiera from using her magic to heal herself. She snapped her head to the cell's entrance when a wolf padded in, dragging a cloaked guard.

The wolf tossed the bleeding guard into the center of the room. Stacy bent over him, grabbed his cloak, and hauled him up. "What are you doing here?"

Despite his pain, the guard produced a crooked smile. "My king will tear your world apart root by fucking root. He has already begun. The magic in this world will be his."

Stacy's rage flared. "Where is he?"

"Stacy..." Miles began cautiously.

She ignored him. *"Where. Is. He?"*

The fae smirked. "He's waiting for you in the throne room, Anastasia Drakethorn. He has wanted to see a dragon for a very long time."

"There is someone at the gate," a gravelly voice stated from the door of Amy's office. She glanced at the werewolf, one of those who'd stayed behind to guard the estate while the others were away. She'd spent the past couple of hours researching for Stacy and was glad to have a break. She stood, wondering who was visiting at this time of night. A glance at the clock told her it was after 11:00.

The werewolf went with her. Amy pulled on a wool coat at the door before stepping onto the snow-dusted sidewalk. Someone wearing a coat and hat was at the gate. Amy approached the person with apprehension. The Thorn house and grounds were covered in illusion magic to make the place look uninhabited. Only magicals could see through the illusion or humans like Amy who were permitted to do so.

She recognized him only from her research. What the hell was Damien Hartwell doing here? As far as Amy knew, he did not possess the magic to see the estate for what it was.

As she neared the gate with the brawny guard at her side, Damien's eyes swept over her, and an easy smile graced his lips. "You must be a friend of Stacy's."

Amy wasn't sure how she felt about this stranger mentioning Stacy's name as if they were old friends. "Who are you?" she asked despite knowing his name. Let him think he wasn't important enough for Stacy to mention him.

He dipped his head in greeting. "Damien Hartwell. I met Stacy the other day. This is her home, right? I am heading back to DC and was passing this way. I had hoped to see her before I left the state to discuss opportunities to work together." As he spoke, his eyes roamed past Amy. He didn't seem to notice the burly bodyguard.

"It is very late," Amy replied coolly. "Stacy already retired."

Damien's eyes slid back to Amy and glinted in amusement. Stacy had not told anyone outside her inner circle her plans for the night, but did he know she was gone?

"I will let her know you stopped by," Amy added. "If she wishes to contact you, she will."

Damien bristled. "Very well. Have a good night, miss." He walked toward his car, which was several yards from the gate, still running as though he had either expected the gate to be opened so he could drive in or that he would have to leave soon.

Perhaps Damien Hartwell had come to find out if Stacy did live here. *I confirmed that for him. Shit.*

Hartwell glanced over his shoulder, but not at Amy or the werewolf. His eyes fastened on the house, and he looked puzzled. He was probably confused by its dilapidated state. If only he knew what it truly looked like.

Amy's mind whirred. Damien couldn't have been "passing by" on his way to DC. He had stopped by on purpose. There was something off about him, Amy thought as she turned back to the house.

Before she made it to the porch, headlights swept across the yard. She turned, squinting. She recognized the car as being from Khan's estate. She waited until the person parked and slid out of the driver's seat. "Reginald? What are you doing here?"

Khan's butler approached the gate as Amy and the werewolf did. Amy nodded at the guard to open the barrier. "Thank you," Reginald murmured. "Is Stacy here? Of course she isn't. I forgot about poor Kiera."

Reginald did not seem to be himself. He was usually composed and congenial. This version of Reginald was shaken. "What happened?" she asked.

"May we speak inside?"

Amy led the butler into the house. The werewolf remained by the gate in case anyone else came to visit. Once inside, Amy took her favorite seat in the living room, an armchair by the roaring fire. Reginald was too agitated to sit. He paced before her. "I received an alarming piece of news this evening, Miss Greentree." He produced a folded piece of paper from inside his coat. "An old friend of mine and acquaintance of Lord Drakethorn's came to the estate this evening with this letter, wondering if I knew anything about the event Stacy was holding tonight. I told him that as far as I knew, Stacy wasn't holding any event."

He handed the paper to Amy. Frowning, she read its contents.

Dear Mr. Grove,

Please accept this formal invitation to my event tomorrow evening, November 20th, in celebration of recent legal victories and the progression of unity for all paranormals in our community. I look forward to discussing with you and the other guests ways we can improve our community together. I have invited you because we share a similar vision of freedom in a world that seeks to trample us. Please refer to the enclosed dress code, RSVP options, and address.

Yours truly,

Anastasia Drakethorn

"Stacy didn't send this!" Amy exclaimed. "She would not say something like 'freedom in a world that seeks to trample us.' She doesn't use rhetoric like that."

Reginald's grave expression added to Amy's alarm. "I am afraid that Miss Anastasia walked into a trap and that my friend nearly did the same, as well as other members of the established magical community. He chose not to attend when I revealed that the letter wasn't from Stacy."

"Who did this, and why?" Amy wondered, concern causing a crease between her eyebrows.

"I don't know who sent it, but Stacy has many enemies. Maybe some banded together."

Amy balled the letter up and tossed it on the floor. "I must warn her."

"I will contact Lord Drakethorn, though I do not expect a speedy response."

Amy nodded. "That is a good idea. Thank you for bringing this to me."

The butler nodded and left Amy to contemplate the night's events. She didn't think Damien's appearance was a coincidence.

What the hell was going on?

Stacy did not hear her friend's warnings, only the wild thumping of her heart as she burst from Kiera's cell. She would find a way to the fae king, wherever the hell he was lurking, and end this before he could do anything worse.

Ethan followed her, as did the witches. Nox had stayed with Rowan and Miles to heal Kiera. The wolves trailed the witches to protect the group. She was vaguely aware of what Ethan was saying, but she did not allow herself to heed his words.

A hand grazed her arm. She twisted to find Ethan behind her, breathing labored. "Stacy—"

"I will make him pay," she interrupted, her voice sharper than she had intended.

Ethan's mouth formed a grim line. Stacy knew her eyes were now gold instead of green. She wanted to take dragon form, but this space was too confined to do so. She sensed more of the sickening dark magic and knew she was close to the source. He was still here. Thoughts and questions swirled her mind.

Why did this fae king think he could come and take whatever he pleased? He had a world of his own to ravage and should have left theirs the fuck alone. Stacy imagined engulfing him in flames, turning him to ash drifting on the wind. He wanted to see a dragon? He fucking would.

Stacy reached a winding staircase and began her ascent, aware that Ethan, four of the witches, and the wolves were following her. There had to be hundreds of stairs. As she climbed, Stacy had wondered if they would ever end. The muscles in her legs were burning when she reached the top and strode into a room with a stone throne on a dais.

On that throne was a man in a gold robe, silver hair streaming to his waist. He wore a crooked smile beneath an elegant crown of twisted branches and jewels. The fae king, whatever the fuck his name was. Kiera had never told her, and Stacy had not asked.

Stacy marched toward him, eyes locking on the king's. She halted after a few steps, however, and her gut twisted.

Six bodies lay on the floor, blood pouring from their wounds. Their limbs bent at unnatural angles, and their open mouths and wide eyes spoke of the terror and agony they'd experienced before their lives ended. They were dressed in attire worthy of a gala or a ball, their clothes ruined by their blood.

"Fucking hell," Ethan muttered as he knelt before one of the bodies. "I know this man, or I *knew* him."

Stacy recognized him as well. She'd met the high-ranking member of the magical community at an event a few months ago. Why was he here, and why was he *dead*?

She jerked her head toward the throne to confront the king, but the stone seat was empty. *"Where are you?"*

Agatha came to her side, placing comforting hands on her arms. "Stacy." Her voice was soft yet held warning.

Stacy didn't listen. Her gaze went to Ethan, who had noticed something in the man's hand and was prying it from his cold fingers. He opened it and paled as he read the paper's contents. "Stacy!"

"What is it?" she demanded, tearing away from Agatha. Ethan stood and handed her the letter. Stacy noted her name at the bottom, a near-perfect forgery, then read the contents. She could not believe it. These people had come expecting her and whatever and a grand event, not their deaths. "Kiera was the bait to lure me here."

"And the fae king—" Ethan started.

Stacy swallowed hard, nodding. "He framed me for murder."

CHAPTER THIRTEEN

Amy had not realized she'd dozed off at her desk until the front door opened and people tramped in, jolting her awake. She glanced at the clock; it was three in the morning. She headed downstairs despite her groggy state.

Rowan was carrying a battered, unconscious Kiera. Relief swept through Amy, but it was quickly dampened by Rowan's grim expression. Miles wore the same expression. Rowan and Miles rushed upstairs, breezing past Amy like they didn't see her. She didn't mind when one of the coven witches did the same, passing like a shadow.

Amy looked around. The other four coven witches and the five Graytails trailed in next. Stacy and Ethan entered last, looking both furious and sad. Amy was dying to know what had happened and to share Damien's strange visit and what she had learned from Reginald with Stacy. She'd tried to contact Stacy and warn her that she was walking into a trap, but nothing had worked. Amy's relief at seeing her friend safe and uninjured was immense.

Stacy turned to the wolves and the witches. "Thank you all for your help. We would have died without you." Her voice lacked its normal conviction. Amy wondered if it was exhaustion or something else.

The Graytails nodded, promised to inform their Alpha of what had happened, and left. The witches briefly murmured to Stacy and Ethan before dispersing to guest rooms, too exhausted to drive home. Though no one appeared injured, the group had clearly taken a beating. It must have been nice to have magic and heal quickly. Kiera hadn't been so lucky. Amy dreaded hearing what had happened to her.

Stacy finally saw Amy. Her shoulders sagged as if she were on the brink of collapse or tears, and a dozen emotions flickered over her face. She muttered "Amy" as if her friend's name were a lifeline.

Amy took her hand. "Let's go upstairs and talk."

Stacy felt like she was sleepwalking.

She didn't know what time it was, only that it was still dark outside. She knew that they had come up to Amy's study and settled into comfortable leather chairs. She knew Ethan had remained downstairs to fix food and find them something to drink. She heard Amy's comforting voice say, "Tell me what happened."

Stacy began with the details that were easier: Miles creating the tunnel and their infiltration into the castle, finding Kiera, and learning from the fae guard about the fae king's presence on their world. Amy's expression grew troubled, and Stacy stumbled as she told her friend what had happened next. The bodies, the disappearing king, and the realization that she'd been framed.

"I knew it was a trap, but I still went." Stacy's voice wobbled. "It was a set-up from the beginning, and he used Kiera, his fucking *daughter*, to lure me in."

Amy touched Stacy's arm. "You would have been framed by

those letters whether you went or not. You brought our friend back, and that is what matters. You aren't wrong for walking into that trap. You would be a lesser woman if you had chosen not to rescue Kiera."

Stacy knew Amy was right, but she couldn't force her heart to believe it. Tears pricked her eyes. All she could think of were those lost lives, what had happened to Kiera, and not being aware of the fae king's presence. *I should have been paying attention. I should have prepared. How did we not notice something was amiss?*

Her voice broke. "I've never felt this lost and confused. I've always been able to handle the threats I face. I thought Lenny Dolos and Victor Corbinelli were bad, but this…" She trailed off, unable to compose words. Exhaustion gripped her body and dug its fingers into her mind.

"You're allowed to feel lost and confused."

Am I? Stacy wondered. If she could not defeat the trespassing king, who would? She needed to learn more about his intentions. That crooked smile on his perfect face would haunt her dreams.

Stacy continue, "I should have known this was coming. Maybe it's not a real threat and I was stupid not to see it. I should have called my father the moment we learned Kiera had been taken, but I let my pride hold me back. I didn't want to need his help."

Amy rose, then knelt before her and took her hands. "You cannot blame yourself for this, and Reginald contacted your father."

Stacy raised her head and met Amy's gaze. "Regi was here?"

Amy told Stacy about the butler's visit and the invitation, then told her about Damien's appearance. Stacy's brow furrowed. "Damien wasn't simply 'passing by.' He came with a purpose. I want to know what the hell it was."

"It *was* strange," Amy agreed. "We need answers."

She had forgotten about Damien Hartwell when she'd learned Kiera had been taken.

"The fae king must see you as a threat," Amy added. "Your father too. He wants you out of the way before he does what he wants on this world. He must have learned of your exploits and knows better than to take you out from the shadows. He wants to turn the paranormal community against you."

Stacy's heart ached, but she nodded. "What better way to do that than by making it look like I murdered some of them?"

The following silence was heavy and solemn. It was a silence Stacy had not felt since the death of their friend Spencer. She also thought about Luna. How many more lives would be lost before her enemies were vanquished?

She was so fucking tired.

Amy blew out a breath. "You need to rest, Stacy. When Kiera can talk, we will ask her what she knows."

She was right. The fae who wanted to kill Stacy and take over their world was Kiera's father. *I bet she wishes he was not.* Ethan appeared a moment later with food and tea, but she felt too sick to eat, with the images of those corpses burned into her mind.

Ethan squeezed her shoulder. "It's okay. Drink some of this, then go to bed."

She was distantly aware of drinking hot tea, then Ethan's arms. When he tucked her into bed, slumber took her under.

When Kiera opened her eyes, she was not in a cell. Not only was she not in a cell, but she also wasn't suspended from chains that shut off her magic. The first rays of dawn were peeking through the curtains, and she was lying on a comfortable bed. *Her* bed.

She was face-down with her head turned on the pillow. The position confused her until she remembered her shredded back. Whoever had placed her here had been careful not to further agitate the wounds. Memories came rushing back. She'd been whipped. Kiera had lost count of how many times they'd lashed her back before she blacked out. She remembered taunts, mockery, and questions. She hadn't answered, as far as she could remember.

Kiera tried to move, but her back screamed in protest. A woman wearing a simple black dress that fell to her feet wafted into the room as if sensing she was awake. Her ebony hair was cut to chin level, and she wore a placid expression. Her small white hands were quick, gentle, and efficient. Kiera remembered those hands through hours of being almost asleep but aware that someone was tending to her.

She'd assumed it was a fae healer closing up the wounds in her back so they could be opened again, but she now realized that had not been the case since this woman was not fae. The silent woman picked up a bowl and applied herbs ground to a paste to the wounds on Kiera's back—one of the coven members who was a healer. *Shadowy like me,* Kiera thought.

She didn't care that the healer didn't speak. She was skilled; Kiera could tell by how she applied the herbs. It occurred to her that no one else except her would have known how to heal her.

Tears filled Kiera's eyes. They had come for her and brought her home. She was safe.

Her relief faded when she remembered that her father was on the human world and had disastrous plans for it. She had to tell the others, and they had to find a way to defeat him. The mere thought of trying exhausted her.

Alerion Thraxius had never been defeated.

The witch finished with her back and left the room. Kiera still could not move, but the scent of the herbs lulled her toward sleep, and she let it take her. Sleeping let her forget her troubles.

When she awoke the second time, there was a cup of tea on her bedside table, steam curling from the surface. That told her the witch had left it not long ago. The sun was stronger, but it was still morning. Kiera tried moving again, and she was able to turn her head. That was how she discovered she wasn't alone. Rowan was curled up beside her, fast asleep. The lines in his face had smoothed, and he breathed deeply.

Kiera couldn't help her sob of relief, and tears slipped from her eyes, wetting her cheeks. Rowan lifted his head, his voice raspy when he spoke. "Kiera."

She felt his fingers on her cheek as if he needed to touch her to believe she was home. She needed it too. The sound of her name on his lips made more tears form. "Tell me this isn't a dream or some torturous fantasy my father put into my mind," Kiera whispered.

"If you are dreaming, so am I." Rowan produced a faint smile and pressed a kiss to her brow. When he drew back, tears glistened in his eyes. "You are home. This is real."

Kiera returned his smile. "I would very much like to drink that tea."

She hated being helpless, but she let Rowan turn her over and prop her against the pillows. Her wounds barked, but she clenched her teeth against the pain. Rowan had moved her gently and handed her the tea. It was rich with herbs, made by the same witch who was attending her.

"What happened?" Kiera asked after sipping the tea.

Grief flickered over Rowan's face. Kiera was afraid of what he would say. "Did everyone make it out?"

He nodded. "But things did not go as planned. The fae king tricked us."

Kiera appreciated that he said "the fae king" instead of "your father." As for the trickery, she wasn't surprised. She prodded him to share what he knew. Rowan began with their infiltration and what the fae guard had said to Stacy when they located Kiera in her cell. He told her about the rescue, the bodies in the throne room, the fae king's disappearance, and the letter.

Kiera was speechless when he finished. She had expected

some vile hoax from her father, but not this. She burned with rage at the thought of Stacy being framed, then blamed herself.

Rowan read the thoughts on her face and took her hand, swiping his thumb over where the chains had rested. "Do not blame yourself, Kiera. There is a lot of self-blame going on at the moment."

Before Kiera could tell him how she felt, three people entered the room. The first was Stacy, smiling despite the hollows around her eyes. "Kiera, I'm so glad to see you awake."

Amy came in behind her, looking relieved. Ethan strode in last, nodding a solemn greeting to her and Rowan.

"I heard what happened," Kiera told them. "This is a good time to tell you my side of things." She shifted, wincing at the pain in her back. "My father is a cruel and proficient trickster, but his ego is so big that he cannot help but expose his plans. I'm sure he did not tell me his full agenda, but I know why he came here."

Kiera told about her abduction and the time in the dungeon, leaving out parts of her torture. She couldn't bear seeing pain and rage on Rowan's face. She shared how she had been brought before her father and all that he'd said. "They have sucked all life and magic from the land on my homeworld, and they cannot revive it without taking magic from another world."

"From here," Ethan murmured.

"From here," Kiera agreed.

Stacy sank onto the chair that the healing witch had used when attending to Kiera through the night. "And I am in the way. That is why he framed me."

"He wants to weaken your standing with your allies," Kiera confirmed. "And when you are weak, he will strike. There's more. My father would not have come here unless he believed he could defeat anyone who stood against him on this world. He is too proud to take that risk. Someone of high standing must have helped him and promised him power or whatever the hell they thought he would want. They probably knew where I was and told him. Then they used me as bait."

"To get to me," Stacy murmured.

"He probably also wanted to torture me again. It has been centuries since he had the pleasure." She told them about Cyprian's betrayal and death, earning grimaces from her listeners.

"My father's name is Alerion Thraxius," Kiera finished. "He intends to spread fear across this world and defeat its inhabitants so he can take whatever he wishes." Magic, lives, slaves. The list went on. "He has many other secrets that I am not aware of, so we must be careful as we move forward. We must gather our allies and tell them what has happened before rumors of the murders reach them."

Kiera was right; they had to move quickly. Stacy stood and turned to Rowan. "Send word to all our friends. Amy, please go with him so it gets done quicker."

The pair nodded and left the room. Rowan cast one last glance at Kiera. Her heart ached when he left. "Where is Miles?"

"With the Graytails," Stacy answered. "Pleading for the pack to join us."

"He probably doesn't have to plead," Ethan remarked. "When they hear what happened, the Alpha will be so enraged that she will pledge their aid to us."

Kiera hoped that was true, but she'd seen how fear divided people. Would the pack succumb to it? If anyone could bolster their confidence in Stacy, it was Miles.

"We wanted to talk to you about something else too," Ethan added. He told Kiera what he had discovered about Malabbra. "I am wondering if you learned anything about the dark world when you lived among the fae. Did you ever hear of creatures slipping out of Malabbra onto other worlds?"

"I didn't," Kiera answered. "That doesn't mean it didn't happen, though. It is very possible that it did. Where such creatures are lurking, though, I do not know."

Rowan came back into the room before Ethan could ask another question. He directed his attention to Stacy. "We are receiving calls from all sides. The community found out about the murders and connected them to you."

Stacy's expression hardened. Kiera clenched her blanket. "And?" Stacy asked.

"Some believe you are being framed," Rowan answered. "Many aren't convinced you didn't do it, though. They say all wealthy, powerful people eventually turn corrupt, and you finally have."

Kiera could see the narrative. Paranormals who'd witnessed Stacy dismantling the underworld for months might believe she'd done it so she alone would sit on the throne, which couldn't be farther from the truth. They had to show them who Stacy truly was and reveal the enemy behind the veil, but it wasn't going to be easy.

"I might have to deal with legal action soon," Stacy mused. "We have to prepare ourselves. What did our allies say?"

"Elentya and the Shinnecock are on our side, and Miles is talking to the Graytails," Rowan replied. "As for everyone else, it's complicated."

They had allies, though.

Stacy straightened her shoulders and lifted her head. "I will meet with Damien Hartwell and figure him out. I might end up needing help from the FBI. Amy will come with me. Rowan, would you contact his assistant?"

Rowan agreed and left the room again.

Amy reentered while Rowan was leaving and overheard Stacy's decision to visit Damien. "Are we taking another trip? I didn't mind the last one."

Stacy shot her friend a faint, tired smile. "Damien is driving home now. It doesn't make sense to visit him today when he might not even be there yet."

Amy smiled. "I have a way to pass the time, then."

Stacy arched a brow. "What's that?"

"I don't know about you, but with everything going on, I haven't done a lick of Christmas shopping." She grinned at Kiera. "What do you think about a girls-only shopping trip this afternoon?"

CHAPTER FOURTEEN

Kiera wasn't in good enough condition to shop, so Stacy and Amy set out for the nearby village of Briar Ridge. The village had little activity except in the summer and around holidays when wealthy estate owners came for vacation. The village had one street lined with shops, boutiques, and cafes that were open until mid-afternoon.

It had taken some convincing on Amy's part for Stacy to go. Her mind was a torrent of concerns over recent affairs, but Amy insisted that it was needed. "Kiera could use some cheering up. Let's get her a treat and bring it back," was the comment that persuaded Stacy to go.

"We can grab lunch and shop for an hour," Stacy decided. "This afternoon, Ethan and I are meeting with the coven to initiate our new member."

If she still wants to be part of it, Stacy added inwardly.

Amy looped her arm through Stacy's on the way to the car. "You have every right to feel down, but Alerion Thraxius has no concept of love or buying gifts for one's friends. We do, and we should always make time for the small things."

Stacy gave Amy an appreciative smile. "You always remind me of what is important."

During their venture, Stacy fought off waves of guilt as if she had truly murdered those people. It took all her focus to think of Christmas gifts and her friends. It would be their first Christmas together and her first holiday season at the Thorn estate. Despite her looming enemies, Stacy intended to make it one to remember.

She ran through the list in her mind. New gloves and boots for Miles, new journals for Ethan for his research results, a bottle of Rowan's favorite wine, a whetstone and a cleaning kit for Kiera's knives, and a new inkwell for her father, who needed no gifts and insisted she give him nothing. Stacy wanted to get something for each member of the coven and send gifts to the Graytails as well.

Eventually, she was able to put aside her guilt and worry and focus on the task at hand. Stacy stole to the back of a shop when she saw a pair of shoes Amy would like and purchased them while her friend was distracted. When they finished, the back seat of Stacy's car was full.

Amy grinned. "We did damage to our bank accounts and boosted the economy in Briar Ridge."

Stacy smiled, glad that no one had noticed them, or if they had, they'd ignored the dragon heiress in their midst. The shop owners were human, as far as Stacy could tell. They might have known she was the wealthy Drakethorn heir, but they had not heard about her recent trouble.

It must be nice to be blissfully ignorant. She hadn't been since she went back to her father, but she didn't regret it.

"Stacy, what's wrong?" Amy asked.

Stacy became aware of a seatbelt clicking and the hum of the music Rowan preferred, which was classical. "Let's go home," Stacy responded with as she started the car and pulled down the street.

The bare trees passed in a blur, and Stacy enjoyed the feeling of her mother's locket against her skin. When she was close to her home, the magic locket warmed her chest. It was as if the locket knew she needed reassurance.

You have people on your side, she reminded herself. *Even those who are no longer here.*

The coven had spent the night at the estate with intentions of returning home following Claire's initiation ritual. When Stacy returned from the shopping trip, the whole coven was waiting for her in the library. Ethan was quietly conversing with Claire by the fireplace.

When Stacy entered, all eyes went to her. Everyone was solemn, so Stacy wasn't the only one feeling the weight of last night's incident. Though she carried more than anyone else, their presence was a comfort. Stacy halted a few feet from Claire. "I trust you are aware of recent events."

Claire nodded. "We heard the rumors, and Rowan contacted my father and told him what had happened. Ethan filled me in on the details when I arrived. Do not think for one moment that I plan on backing out, Ms. Drakethorn. I want to see this through, given this threat."

"He wants me dead," Stacy replied. "You don't have to be involved if you do not feel ready."

Claire looked grim. "What happens if he defeats you? The rest of us will be next, whether we are ready or not. I want to fight at your side."

Stacy admired the young woman's courage and conviction. She turned to the other witches. "What does everyone else think?"

"If she wants to, I say let her," Emile offered. Agatha nodded.

"I like her spark," Diana commented from her perch by the window. Demetrius, who was leaning against the wall, nodded.

Nox drifted out of the shadows, and her black eyes met Claire's. The young woman held the other witch's gaze, unfaltering. Finally, Ethan said, "Let's do it." He gave Stacy an encouraging nod.

Stacy returned her attention to Claire, feeling hopeful. "All right, then. Let's begin, shall we?"

She and Ethan led the witches toward the ritual stones at the back of the walled portion of the estate. The stones were arrayed in a circle, with the Visionary stone in the center. Stacy stood by it with Ethan while the others moved to the stones that represented their roles. Ethan motioned for Claire to step onto the stone across from where they stood. If the circle was a clock, she was at 6:00.

"I trust that you have learned and practiced the Rite of Grounding and Centering," Ethan stated. The ritual involved connecting with the energy of the earth to remain balanced and focused. Since it served as the foundation for the coven's magical work, a new member must know it.

Claire nodded. "I learned it years ago."

Ethan gave her an encouraging smile. "Good. Then all we must do today is perform the Rite of the Covenant, which is a solemn pact between you, our prospective member, and those who already belong."

Ethan glanced at the other witches, seeking agreement. Emile, Agatha, Demetrius, Diana, and Nox nodded. They were ready. "Each witch will activate their stone using their magic, flowing into yours. You will then use your magic to fuse with ours until your stone activates, allowing you access to both the magic contained within the stones and connection to the rest of us. Any questions?"

Claire shook her head. "I'm ready."

Stacy had observed the young woman throughout. She was

attentive to what Ethan said, eager to learn, and determined to get it right on the first go.

"If this takes a few attempts, that is fine," Ethan assured her. He grinned at Stacy. "Some of us had a steep learning curve."

Stacy rolled her eyes. "Let's get on with it."

Di snickered. Dem provided a wry smile.

"One other thing," Ethan said before they began. "I hope you have a sense of humor, Claire. You won't fit in otherwise."

She smiled. "We'll find out, won't we?"

"First, the Rite," Stacy inserted. She smiled at Claire, green eyes bearing flecks of gold. "Show us what you've got, witch."

Kiera stretched her legs first, then swung them over the side of the bed. Other than being stiff, they worked fine. She placed one foot on the floor, then the other. The trouble began when she tried to stand. Her back stretched, and pain flared. Kiera winced, but she was determined to stand. She held onto the headboard and pushed herself up.

This was fucking embarrassing.

Days ago, she had taken out a skilled drug cartel assassin in an alley and disposed of his body. Now she could barely get out of bed without help.

"You should be resting," said a calm voice from the doorway. She turned to see Rowan leaning against the doorframe, arms folded. Exhaustion was heavy in his eyes.

"You should too," Kiera replied, still upright. She wished she could let go of the headboard, but she couldn't seem to loosen her grip.

Someone had pulled the curtains open, and Kiera could see the last of its rays leaking through the naked trees on the grounds.

"You can't rest standing up," Rowan countered.

"Neither can you."

He gave her a half-smile. Nox, the healing witch, had come to her room every few hours to apply more salve to her back. Kiera expected it to be fully healed within a few days, but she wished it could be sooner. She wanted to get better so she could face her father. No way in hell would she let the others go against him without her.

Rowan strode over to her and looped her arm around his neck, then supported her by wrapping an arm around her waist. She'd been intimate with Rowan before in a number of ways, but not like this. He settled her onto the bed. "On my watch, you'll stay in bed."

Kiera glowered. "It's fucking boring."

He flicked her nose. "I know."

"Tell me what has been happening."

Rowan shared that he had called Damien Hartwell's assistant and arranged for Stacy to meet with him tomorrow. Right now, she and Ethan were initiating a new witch into their coven. As for the paranormal community and their questions about the murders, they'd chosen not to say anything for the time being. "Stacy wants to wait until her father returns or at least contacts her."

Kiera leaned over and kissed him. When she pulled back, she whispered, "I knew you would come for me. I hoped you wouldn't since I couldn't bear the thought of them hurting you too." Her voice cracked on the final words.

Rowan folded her hands in his. "I will always find you, Kiera." Raw love flickered through his eyes. "I was more afraid than I have ever been when I realized who had taken you. Miles was too, though he might not show it."

"Miles wears every emotion on his gardening gloves," Kiera reminded him, smiling faintly.

"There is something you're not saying, Kiera. You have been holding it in since you awoke this morning."

Kiera considered her words. "I am afraid of what my father will do." Her voice was weak; she hated that.

Rowan cupped her face in his hands. "I will be at your side no matter what. He will not hurt you again."

It was this loyalty that made her father think she was weak, but Kiera knew it was the opposite: she'd been weak until she came to the human world and made these connections. She might have suffered for it, but she wouldn't die while he was here.

Her father's face flashed through her mind, and she shivered.

CHAPTER FIFTEEN

"This place is a lot more rundown than I expected," Amy murmured. She and Stacy stood before Damien Hartwell's estate.

Stacy had to agree. The grounds were not well-maintained, especially the cracked pavement leading to the front door. Everything about the place seemed glum, even the trees draping their low, leafless branches across the walkway. "Maybe it's prettier in spring?" Stacy wondered.

Rowan had stayed in the car. Stacy had wanted to blow off steam by coming in dragon form, but she did not trust Damien enough to arrive at his house that way. She and Amy had come via her father's private jet. Stacy had not known her father had one until Rowan mentioned it.

"Of course he has a private jet! How do *you* know?" she had demanded that morning.

"Reginald mentioned it once."

Stacy had grumbled that if her father wanted to leave her in charge of everything, he needed to tell her what all there was. Rowan had shrugged in response. "Maybe he forgot."

"About his private jet?"

"He probably has more than one."

Reginald had sent word to Khan about recent circumstances but had yet to receive a response. An hour and a half plane ride later, Stacy, Amy, and Rowan arrived in Washington, DC, and they rented a car to take to the Hartwell estate outside the city. Stacy had insisted that Rowan stay behind with Kiera, but the dryad had protested that Kiera was doing better and had plenty of protection and help at the estate.

"My job is to be your driver and bodyguard. Let me do my job."

Rowan intended to stay with the car in case the meeting went sour and they needed to leave quickly. At the front door, Stacy and Amy were greeted by an old housekeeper who gave them a tight-lipped smile and said the master of the house would be with them shortly. She led them through a dim, dusty hallway to a parlor and left them there without a word.

"This place smells weird," Amy whispered. "And I doubt that housekeeper does much. Did you see how frail she was?" She swiped her finger through dust on a mantle.

Stacy surveyed the room, noting the empty fireplace and the gray curtains parted to allow pale sunlight in. The antique furniture was devoid of comforts such as cushions and blankets, and there were no rugs on the floors. Each step they took was on creaking floorboards, with dust swept into corners. The paintings and photographs on the wall depicted former overseers of this estate. Stacy had the feeling they were staring right into her.

The room was stately and impressive, but it lacked the comforts and cheer of a home. Stacy felt like she was in a museum and should not sit on the furniture.

"Stacy, thank you for waiting." She turned as Damien entered, wearing a congenial smile. His eyes shifted to Amy. "And you've brought a friend!"

"Damien, this is Amy Greentree, a friend of mine and a private investigative journalist. She has covered many of my previous cases."

Amy extended her hand to shake his. "We met briefly the other night, Mr. Hartwell."

"Ah, yes. I want to apologize for that." Damien's eyes shifted from Amy to Stacy, and he seemed to forget to shake her hand. "I know how strange it must have been with me showing up that late at night. I simply didn't want to miss an opportunity to speak to you."

Stacy wanted to believe him, but she had an inkling that he was covering his tracks. Why? Damien motioned to a stiff settee. "Please, make yourself comfortable. My housekeeper is preparing drinks and refreshments. What has brought you to DC, Stacy?" Damien lowered himself to a small sofa opposite the settee as the women sat.

"You, actually," Stacy answered. "Things in New York have recently taken a turn, and I wanted to see what help you could offer."

"Oh? I should have stayed in the city longer then. Perhaps I could have met with you during the day." He laughed.

Stacy tilted her head, observing him in a new light. Damien seemed different now that she was seeing him in his home. He did not seem as if he belonged here, but Amy's research had shown that he had never lived anywhere else. Damien did not fit into the room as Stacy felt she did at the Thorn estate. Rather, Damien wore the room. The house was an accessory to his persona.

A dusty one, Stacy thought. "It was nearly as strange as the letter you sent me, and I wonder about something. Amy told me you weren't certain if I lived at the Thorn estate, yet you sent a letter there, seeming sure it was my home. Why?"

Damien's expression shifted, but the change was fleeting. He composed himself with relative ease. *He realizes he's been caught in a lie*, Stacy thought.

Before she could say anything else, the parlor door creaked open and the housekeeper appeared, holding a tray with cups, saucers, a pot of coffee, and pastries. The tray rattled in her feeble hold. Damien just watched as she set it down and didn't thank her as she shuffled out of the room.

Damien leaned toward the tray and plucked up pastry before his eyes traveled back to Stacy. This time, he observed her from face to toe as if considering her in a new way. "I heard about an incident in the city. Maybe that is what you mean by 'things have taken a turn.' People say six members of your paranormal community were murdered at an event *you* held."

How the hell would he know about that?

A cold glint came into his eyes, and his easy manner vanished. "You are exactly what I thought you were, Stacy Drakethorn: a paranormal terrorist. I am glad you came to me today since the FBI plans to take care of you."

Stacy suddenly felt cold. Amy had reached for a cup to pour coffee but froze, then drew her hand back. Her voice was like ice when she demanded, "What did you say?"

Damien ignored Amy, which pissed Stacy off. "What do you have to say for yourself?"

Don't react, Stacy told herself. She kept her expression mild and tone even. "I had nothing to do with that crime. I was framed."

Damien chuckled as if he'd been told a joke. "By who?"

Stacy opened her mouth to respond but realized how ridiculous it would sound that fae from another world had come here and done it. Would Damien even know what fae were? She waited too long to respond, and Damien laughed again. "If you are going to lie, you need to become better at it."

"The same could be said about you," Amy cut in. "You lied about not knowing where Stacy lived. You knew where her home was both when you sent the letter and when you showed up. Why aren't you keeping your story straight?"

Damien's eyes slid to Amy, and he observed her as if bored by her presence. "I am not the one on trial here, Miss Greentree."

"No one is on trial," Stacy shot back.

"Not yet," was Damien's cool reply. "We are gathering all we need to build a case against you, Stacy."

Her heart thumped as it dawned on her that Damien Hartwell had been against her this entire time. She felt stupid for not seeing it before. "You never wanted to work with me," Stacy accused.

Damien shrugged with forced nonchalance. "I wanted to see how compliant you would be. When it became clear you wouldn't be, I had a reason to investigate you further. I had suspicions about you before, and now there is this matter of mass murder."

His eyes gleamed, as if he'd been waiting for something like this to happen. *As if he knew it was going to happen,* Stacy realized.

Damien leaned forward, intertwining his fingers and fixing Stacy with a penetrating stare. "I know about your involvement in the removal of certain underworld criminals. I also think you are trying to kill members of your paranormal community so that you, and you alone, can sit on the throne."

"You have no proof--" she began.

Damien continued as if he had not heard her. "I wonder where your father is in all of this. Funny that he's run off just as his daughter's grand magical career is getting started. I wonder what crimes *he* is committing while leaving his daughter behind with her mess. Or did he start the mess?"

Stacy was one word away from launching across the room and wrapping her hands around his neck. She reined in her rage, though. Any reaction could be used against her. She turned to Amy. "This meeting was a waste of time. We're leaving."

"Right behind you," Amy replied, shooting Damien a heated glare.

They were in the hallway when Damien called after them, "We'll see one another again soon!"

When Stacy, Rowan, and Amy returned to the Thorn estate that evening, Ethan, Miles, Kiera, and the coven were waiting for them in the library.

Stacy's gaze went to Kiera, surprised and relieved that she was out of bed. Normally, the sidhe fae sat in a dark corner, using discussion time to sharpen her knives. This evening, however, she occupied a seat by the fire and was wrapped in a blanket with a cup of tea balanced on a raised knee.

Nox hovered nearby as if her mere presence would continue to heal Kiera. Kiera's color had returned, and now she merely seemed tired. When they entered, Rowan went to her, dropped onto the sofa beside her, and rested a hand on the tea-free knee. Kiera cast him an appreciative glance before her brows furrowed. "Something happened." It wasn't a question but an observation.

Ethan strode over to Stacy and placed a hand on the small of her back. "It didn't go well, did it?"

"Other than when Damien called me a terrorist and said the FBI would be coming to take care of me, it went splendidly," Stacy replied.

"He's lucky I didn't punch him in the face," Amy grumbled as she dropped into a chair beside Miles.

Stacy turned her attention to the other coven members. Emile and Agatha shared the sofa opposite Kiera and Rowan. Di and Dem had pulled chairs up to a table littered with Ethan's books and scribbled notes. Claire was not present since she had gone home after her initiation to rearrange her life now that she belonged to their coven.

Stacy related what had happened at Damien's estate. "It looks like we have more than one threat on our hands now. The question is, what threat does Damien pose compared to Alerion?"

"He's nothing compared to my father," Kiera ground out, her eyes fixed on the dancing flames in the hearth.

"Still, we don't need the law coming down on us, especially now," Rowan murmured.

The word "we" rang in Stacy's mind. She was being framed, but her friends' association with her might put them in trouble too. Guilt pierced her, but she banished it. None of this was her fault, and her friends had chosen to stand by her. She would welcome their company and assistance.

Agatha cleared her throat. When Stacy turned to her, Agatha looked solemn. "I know you didn't commit murder, Stacy, but this whole ordeal is more than I ever imagined would happen when I joined the coven. I have thought about this a good deal since we left that castle, and I decided it is time for us to part ways."

Stacy's breath caught. Agatha wanted to break the coven's binding oaths. It hit her like a punch to the gut. Why say it now? The timing couldn't have been worse.

The silence in the room was tense before the older witch broke it again with, "For the present time, anyway. I do not want to appear disloyal, but this is... Well, it's too much."

Questions swirled Stacy's mind. Was Agatha afraid of the legal ramifications or what the fae king intended to do? She would escape neither by leaving the coven. Perhaps she just wanted to preserve her life. Stacy couldn't blame the older witch.

Her heart sank. Stacy wished Agatha had come to her and Ethan without an audience. "I am disappointed, Agatha. You have been invaluable to us from the beginning," she said at last, tone solemn. "I understand, though. You may break the binding oaths without consequence."

Agatha stood stiffly and straightened the folds in her dress, aware that many eyes bored into her. The strongest stares came from the other witches. Diana was working hard to keep her remarks behind her teeth. Emile looked to be on the verge of tears, while Demetrius and Nox remained impassive.

Agatha gave Stacy and Ethan a curt nod before addressing the other witches. "I have appreciated my time with you, and I will look back on this with fondness. I will go and gather my things now."

Silence prevailed as Agatha left the room, the sharp clacks of her heels on the floorboards echoing throughout the room. When she was gone, Stacy let out a breath. Ethan put a hand on her shoulder and squeezed.

"I don't understand," Emile stated. "Now, more than ever, it is important for us all to stay together." Emile's expression was a combination of anger and disappointment. Stacy felt the same emotions, but too much had gone on for her to parse them. Agatha's departure was the least of her worries. She wouldn't blame any of them for going, given what happened.

Diana spoke up. "Agatha has always been spineless. I want to be more outspoken about our support for you. Everyone needs to know who stands by you. The rest can fuck off if they have anything bad to say or even *think* about you."

Stacy gave the witch an appreciative smile. "I'm grateful for your support, Di, but I need everyone to remain neutral until we have a better understanding of what is going on. A statement from any of us could radicalize the situation. I want to approach it as I have done with legal matters in the past. If I have to go to court, so be it. It's not like I haven't done it before."

"Except you have never been on trial," Miles pointed out.

Stacy nodded. "I'm not on trial yet. I won't run, and we are not in the wrong. This is only a case in the public's opinion for now, but it is still a case. I won't lose this one." She gave a faint smile. "I've come too far. As for Agatha, I won't hear any negative comments. She isn't spineless, and there is no shame in her departure. I would have preferred her to stay since I don't want anyone in my coven who isn't committed, but I understand her reasons."

Stacy searched the other witches' faces. "If any of you have reservations going forward, I need to know about them."

"None here," Diana inserted. She motioned at her brother, who nodded in agreement. "For either of us."

Nox's silence was confirmation of her intentions to stay, and Emile's comments had made it clear where he stood.

Rowan's gaze met Stacy's, and pride shone in his eyes. He cleared his throat. "To make matters slightly better, I received word on our way back that Elentya and her elves are willing and ready to aid us when needed. If that means making a public statement or fighting by our side, they will do so. Elentya will not soon forget what you did for her home and people, Stacy, and she understands the threat Alerion poses."

"What *we* did," Stacy corrected.

The library door opened, and a werewolf guard from the Graytails who'd stayed with them overnight strode in, his gaze going straight to Stacy. "Ms. Drakethorn, someone is at the gate. Says they're from the FBI."

"Damien?" Amy asked. "No way he got here that fast."

The werewolf shook his head. "Different agents. There are two of them. Said they need to see you, Ms. Drakethorn."

CHAPTER SIXTEEN

Stacy's heart sank.

FBI agents were here at her *home*.

It was easy to guess why they had shown up. She glanced at Ethan, then Rowan, her mind whirring. *What the hell am I supposed to do?* It wasn't like she could pretend she wasn't home since they would just come back. Maybe they had a warrant to search the place.

I have nothing to hide, Stacy reminded herself. *If I don't speak to them, I'll look guilty.* She lifted her chin to address the werewolf. "Show them in here, please."

"Do you think Damien sent them?" Amy asked.

Damien had seemed eager to be part of it, so why hadn't he come with them? She turned to the coven witches and her friends. "I think it is better that none of you are here when I speak to them. No need to put you under further scrutiny."

"The coven should go," Ethan agreed, "but I am staying with you."

"Don't even try to order me away," Rowan added.

"I can attest to the nature of my father's character and the tricks he played," Kiera inserted. "If they are to hear the truth, much of it must come from me."

Stacy eyed Amy, who said, "If everyone else is staying, so am I."

"I will go with Brock to guard the estate while they are here," Miles volunteered. He and the coven witches filed out of the room, each wishing Stacy good luck as they went.

"I'll need it. Here goes nothing," she whispered as the sound of the front door opening reached her. Seconds later, two FBI agents, a man and a woman, entered the room, led in by the werewolf guard.

The woman was nearly six feet tall, with brown skin and dark coils of hair pulled back tightly behind her head. She wore a pale gray pantsuit, and her sharp amber eyes swept the room, taking in its occupants. Recognition flickered in her eyes. She seemed to know who everyone was.

Rowan and Kiera had remained on the sofa by the fire. Amy had moved to the window, and Ethan stood at Stacy's side. The male FBI agent was broad-shouldered and brusque-looking, with a neatly trimmed mustache and dark eyes as observant as his partner's. The woman approached Stacy. "Ms. Drakethorn, thank you for inviting us in. We were hoping to catch you while you were at home." She extended her hand, which Stacy shook, caught off-guard by the woman's friendly manner.

The woman continued. "I am Agent Danica Dravos, and this is my partner, Agent Adam Taylor. We have followed a number of your cases over the past year and have wanted to make your acquaintance. With recent events unfolding, we have found it imperative to come and speak with you."

Stacy willed her pulse to slow down. No need in getting worked up before they accused her of anything. She motioned at the empty sofa and armchairs. "Please, make yourselves comfortable." She signaled to Amy. "We will get you something to drink."

Amy disappeared from the room as Stacy made introductions. "Agent Dravos and Agent Taylor, meet the members of my estate. Rowan manages the day-to-day goings-on, Kiera is the estate's housekeeper, and Ethan is my researcher." Stacy wasn't sure what else to call him without giving away the true nature of his position.

A slow smile spread Agent Davos' lips as she took a seat on the sofa. "Pleased to meet you all, though I am aware, Ms. Drakethorn, that you have severely downplayed your friends' roles."

Stacy tried not to show her alarm at that statement.

Agent Davos turned her gaze upon each of the others in turn before glancing at a file on her lap. "Rowan, we know, is more than the estate manager, and he worked here when your mother, a renowned witch, was the owner. Is that correct?"

Rowan didn't give Stacy time to respond. "That's true, Agent Davos."

"You are a dryad, is that right?"

Rowan nodded curtly, his hold on Kiera's knee tightening. Kiera watched the FBI agents with a predatory focus. Agent Taylor eyed him. Unlike Davos, he'd chosen to stand behind the couch.

"You are *all* paranormals." Agent Davos motioned at the three on the sofa opposite her. "You, Kiera Swiftshadow, are not only a housekeeper of this estate but handle Ms. Drakethorn's vigilante affairs." At least she hadn't said "assassin." Kiera did not respond. "Sidhe and fae," Agent Davos continued. "A rare combination. Interesting." She smiled as if she were amused, but Kiera didn't react. Her expression was unreadable, which would have been disconcerting to most.

Agent Davos seemed unfazed. She turned her attention to Ethan. "You are a witch and much more than a researcher. You helped Ms. Drakethorn develop her magical abilities."

Ethan glanced at Stacy, his expression grim. "That's correct."

"You, Ms. Drakethorn, are far more than a witch. We are aware of your father's nature and can only assume that you share his bloodline, as well as his abilities." Agent Davos refrained from using the word "dragon," but the implication was strong. Before Stacy had a chance to reply, the agent asked, "Where is Miles Ironwood, the groundskeeper? I assume he's handling security with the werewolf we met by the gate."

Shit, Stacy thought. They seemed to know everything.

Agent Davos gestured absently at the library door. "Ms. Greentree is the only non-magical here. I commend you, Ms. Drakethorn on the illusion over your estate. To us, the outside looks to be in a sorry state. I assume that is not the case."

Stacy's mind reeled, but she echoed Ethan's words. "That's correct." She steeled herself for what would come next and added, "I assume you are here because of what Damien Hartwell told you. I am prepared to defend myself. I was not responsible for what happened to those paranormals. We can tell you the full truth and prove that—"

"We are here on account of former Agent Hartwell, but perhaps not in the way you assume," Agent Davos interrupted.

Stacy nearly stumbled over her words. "I'm sorry. Did you say *former* agent Hartwell?"

Agent Taylor spoke up, his voice rumbling across the space between them. "That's right. Hartwell was terminated several months ago following misconduct in cases that involve you, Ms. Drakethorn. Our team was investigating the late Victor Corbinelli and Gregory Hines in relation to the legal matters you were involved in. When we discovered that Hartwell had absconded with documents he wasn't supposed to have, he was terminated. We are now investigating him and those he was aligned with."

Stacy couldn't believe what she was hearing. She lowered

herself onto the nearest seat. Ethan stood behind her chair, looking puzzled. Rowan and Kiera were quiet and watchful. Amy shuffled in a moment later and offered the agents glasses of water.

Agent Davos thanked her before continuing. "I can see you are shocked by all this, Ms. Drakethorn. We know Hartwell recently visited you. We came to ask about the nature of his visit as it relates to our investigation. We assume that Hartwell led you to believe he was still with the FBI. Is that right?"

Amy cursed under her breath.

"That's right," Stacy got out, thoughts still wheeling. "I don't understand, though. You're not here because of the murders?"

Agent Davos had looked impassive until now. A glint of pain came into her eyes. It was gone almost as soon as it had come. "In a way, yes. We do not believe you to be responsible for those. Damien Hartwell has been attempting to frame you for criminal activity for a while, and we believe he had a part in what happened. All the more reason we need to know about your interaction with him."

Stacy forgot how to breathe. This was the last thing she'd expected.

"We will give you answers if you tell us more about Damien's crimes," Ethan offered. "Why is he so interested in Stacy?"

"We cannot speak to his motivations and desires, only what he did," Agent Taylor replied. "He worked alongside several other rogue agents we have recently taken into custody. We are questioning them, but those agents have given very little away. As for Damien, we launched a search for him this morning when we heard about the mass murders. We have evidence that links Hartwell to the people who died."

Agent Davos put a hand to her chest, her voice tightening. "I have a personal interest in this case since one of the people who died is an old friend. She was not a blood relative, but she was like an aunt. She was a high-standing hedge witch in her community. I joined the FBI a decade ago to help paranormals, though I have no magic."

Stacy finally felt like she could relax. Agent Davos clearly had a good sense of character and a moral compass Stacy could work with.

Agent Davos' gaze did not stray from Stacy as she continued. "Other agents reported an hour ago that Hartwell was not at his home, so we wonder if he skipped town. We were able to track his activities to this city, but we assume he has departed by now."

"We saw him at his home a few hours ago," Amy interjected.

Agent Davos' eyes snapped to Amy. "Oh?"

That bastard, Stacy thought. He had done all he could to convince her that he was working alongside the FBI to bring the country's legal apparatus down her. The whole time, he'd been a lying piece of shit. What else had he been deceptive about?

Stacy told the agents everything from the strange letter to their initial meeting and his propositions to his odd arrival in the middle of the night and finally, their meeting today and Damien's threats.

Agent Davos listened intently, and her partner scribbled notes on a pad of paper.

"Beyond that, I know nothing else," Stacy finished. "I found his actions strange, but it never occurred to me that he might be lying about being in the FBI." She gestured at Amy. "My friend's research gave no indication that he had been terminated or that he was being investigated."

"We're keeping all that under wraps for now," Davos responded tightly. "Thank you for all the information. It helps us, and we hope you will be willing to testify against former Agent Hartwell when the time comes."

Stacy nodded, still dazed. The last thing she had expected was to hear that Damien would be going to court and put on trial, not her.

"We will help you with this matter of you being framed,"

Agent Davos added. "It will be a tricky road, but you are innocent until proven guilty." She produced a knowing smile. "As the reputable attorney you are, we know you understand that, Ms. Drakethorn."

Stacy was prepared to leave it there, but a glance from Kiera told her that she couldn't. She was legally in the clear, but that did not mean the road ahead would be less difficult. Damien was one threat, and the fae king was another and much larger one. They needed the FBI's help, so they would make them aware of the rest of the events so far.

"There is a lot more to the matter than I have told you," Stacy continued.

Agent Davos raised a brow.

"We don't suspect Damien Hartwell of framing me, but the truth won't be easy to hear."

Agent Davos looked interested. "Go on. Won't be easy, how?"

"Because it sounds like a load of bullshit," Ethan muttered.

Agent Davos wore an easy smile. "You would be surprised at what I consider a load of bullshit. I have seen a lot in my years as an agent."

Stacy gestured at Kiera. "She was recently abducted by fae from her homeworld at the behest of her father King Alerion Thraxius. He plans to infiltrate our world after I am out of the way. He seems to consider me a threat and wants to do away with me before taking our magic. We know he framed me. The question now is his connection with Damien."

Realization dawned on Stacy as she spoke. Kiera believed that someone of high standing had helped Alerion to slip into their world. What if that had been Damien? How the hell had he managed it?

Kiera spoke up for the first time since the agents had arrived. "We must act quickly. Damien's attempts to frame Stacy are only the tip of the iceberg. None of that shit will matter when my father brings his army through the veil."

She stood with Rowan's assistance, fixing Agent Davos and Agent Taylor in turn with her grim stare. "The FBI and anyone you recruit to help you won't stand a chance against my father if he is able to make good on his scheme." Kiera shifted her focus to Stacy. "We need a plan and fast."

CHAPTER SEVENTEEN

"I don't have a plan," Stacy mused as she lay in bed, staring up at the ceiling. All her life, she'd had a plan, from leaving home and going to law school to every trial. In her law firm, she was the person who had a plan, no matter how complicated the case or what point they were at in their preparations.

Stacy didn't feel right without one.

The blankets moved as Ethan slid in beside her. His mouth brushed her ear. "For the first time in your life."

Stacy turned on her side and propped her fist under her cheek. This wasn't like her attorney days when she stayed up all night devising speeches for court. "I'm serious." Her voice dropped to a whisper. "I don't know how we're going to do it. I don't even know what 'it' is. I don't know that I can wait around for the FBI to get Damien before he does something that royally fucks everything up for me. I also keep thinking, what if the fae king is using Damien as a distraction to do whatever the hell he plans next?"

Ethan stroked her shoulder, his eyes meeting her. "Believe me, I'm as worried about that as you are. Whatever plan we *do* come up with, though, it can't be carried out when you're exhausted. You've had a long day."

They all had. Stacy appreciated that Ethan had used "we." Her friends had made it quite clear in the past months that she wouldn't do anything alone, no matter how hard she tried to exclude them sometimes as a way to protect them.

Then why did it feel like it was? It was her legacy at risk, as well as their lives. It was she who'd been framed and was on trial in the court of public opinion for the deaths of those magicals.

That night felt like an eternity ago. Her mid-morning venture to Damien's home felt the same way. Ethan wrapped Stacy in his arms and pressed her back to his chest. "Sleep now. We'll meet with everyone tomorrow and decide what to do."

Stacy's mind turned over possibilities for several minutes, but finally, Ethan's easy breathing and the thump of his heart lulled her to sleep. She hoped for a dreamless rest, with no images of those the fae king had killed or his murderous, smirking face.

Hours later, Stacy woke with a start. She did not know at first what had awakened her, but then she registered a commotion outside. Ethan bolted up seconds after she did, asking groggily, "What is that?"

Stacy rushed to the window that overlooked the back of the grounds and heard cries of alarm. The moon shone through the trees, illuminating the space. Among the shadows, she glimpsed figures colliding with one another. Her heart lurched at the sight of the estate guards shifting into their wolf forms and launching at dark-cloaked figures that seemed to materialize out of thin air. Not far from the wolves stood Miles, flinging up a wall of vines against the attackers. One such attacker flung a bolt at him. Magicals, all of them.

Stacy's heart raced. Who were these trespassers, and how had they gotten onto the grounds? Ethan flew out of the room, and Stacy grabbed the boots by the door and shoved her feet into them before she reached the first floor. There, they nearly collided with the other witches. Everyone knew what to do. They hurried to the back door and out onto the grounds, magic at their fingertips. Nox kept to the shadows, prepared to step in and heal whoever needed to.

Ethan, Emile, and Stacy lunged at the nearest cloaked figures, forming orbs of magical energy in their palms. Dem and Di raised shields and enforced everyone in strong, pulsing magic. Stacy just had to get those damn bastards off her property.

Stacy flung a flaming orb at the nearest attacker. The creature gave a guttural growl as the fire singed his fur. It was a werewolf. Stacy wondered if she had attacked an ally, but he twisted, and she saw his face. His fur was black, unlike the Graytails', and his eyes blazed red, a clear sign that he was not in his right mind. He was acting on pure instinct and bloodlust. Stacy flung another orb, and he howled as the flames engulfed him.

"Stacy!" someone called. *Rowan.* "Behind you!"

She heard another wolf snarl and ducked. Rowan's ax, blazing with magic, sailed over her head and split the wolf's skull with a sickening thud. Stacy whirled, her shield still active, thanks to the twins. The wolf lay on the ground, blood flowing from the crack. Rowan marched over and withdrew his ax, looking grim. Stacy gave him a nod and spun toward another attacker.

Stacy was not able to tell what it was until it launched at her, flinging bolts from wrinkled fingers. The magic slammed into her shield, which, despite being battered, held. Stacy flung back her magic, and the old witch's robe caught fire. Her howl of agony was no different from the one Stacy had heard the werewolf utter moments ago.

Her coven defended themselves against more wolves, witches, and other paranormals of species Stacy had not yet identified. Rowan wielded his ax and Miles' vines snaked across the ground, catching the infiltrators around their ankles and waists and dragging them into the ground as it opened up.

Stacy flung an orb into the chest of another attacker, sending it stumbling back as Miles opened the ground. The earth closed, trapping them as their screams rang out. She whirled, the attack was over. There was no one left to question. How were they supposed to find out who these people were and why they'd come? *Shit.*

The coven and Rowan and Miles were breathing hard. Stacy was sucking in deep breaths of cold air that stung her lungs. Rowan's ax hung at his side, dripping blood, and she realized she was covered in it.

"Who the hell were they?" Diana asked as she gazed at the bodies littering the ground.

Ethan went to one of the fallen figures and bent to examine it. "Shit. This one is a vampire. The others were witches and wolves."

"A few were shifters," Miles offered. "Another was sidhe, and one was half-fae, half-elf."

"Some look human, so they could be anything," Emile observed.

"Why the hell did they come here?" Diana asked.

Stacy spotted Nox moving toward a Graytails pack member who was leaning against a tree, groaning. Aside from him, no one had been injured.

"They're assassins. Someone sent them here," Ethan posited.

Who? Damien? The fae king? Someone else?

"This attack was messy," Rowan rumbled. "I don't think the fae were behind this. They wouldn't have hired a group of assassins and told them to go at it. They all came here to kill us, but they weren't working together."

"Except to infiltrate the place," Dem interjected. "They slipped through easily enough."

Miles nodded in agreement. "We didn't know they were here until they were upon us."

Skilled assassins, then, but not skilled enough to take on the number the number of defenders on the estate. They had been lucky.

"If not fae, who? Hartwell?" Ethan wondered.

"Could be," Rowan replied. "I think these were assassins hired by underworld crooks. Whether they are with Damien, we can't know."

Stacy took a deep breath to steady herself. That made sense. Given recent events, the enemies still squirming over the vacant underworld throne might have seized the opportunity to strike while they could. "If it is true that they joined forces against me, Damien, Alerion, or both will use them in one big assault before long." Maybe this was a warning of what was to come. Stacy thought something else was in play just out of her sight and reach.

She turned to Rowan. "Call Elentya and the elves and ask them to come here. We will need the backup." Rowan nodded and went inside.

Miles was next. "I'll deal with the bodies, then reinforce the wards in case there are more out there."

Stacy eyed Demetrius and Diana. "You two go with Miles. I want you on guard for the rest of the night."

The witches nodded and trailed after Miles. Ethan, who was standing close to Stacy, faced her. "I'm going in to check on Kiera and Amy."

"I'll go with him," Emile added.

Stacy lingered under the starry sky for a moment to calm down. The adrenaline in her veins kept the cold at bay. The attack had come far too close for comfort. She followed the others into the house and met Rowan in the hallway. His face was pale, and he was holding the phone. Stacy's heart rate increased. "What's wrong? Did something happen to the elves?"

"Elentya and her people are fine. Reginald called. Your father's estate was attacked. Stacy…"

"What?" she pressed, voice shaking.

Rowan swallowed. "It's Torin. They killed him."

Stacy's heart was heavy as she passed through the gate.

Bodies covered the grounds in front of the house, about the same number that had attacked her estate. Stacy put a hand to her mouth as tears welled in her eyes. She spotted Esme leaning over one. The old woman was weeping.

Stacy felt as though her heart would crack from her sorrow. She wondered if she was sleepwalking in a nightmare as she approached Torin's body. She felt like she was floating above the scene, unable to do anything. She might be powerful, but she couldn't turn back time or reverse death.

She was vaguely aware of Rowan and Ethan behind her. Rowan had driven them to the estate, but Stacy remembered nothing of the journey. She knelt at Esme's side and touched the woman's shoulder to offer what comfort she could but also to steady herself.

Torin's eyes were closed, and blood poured from a gaping wound in his chest. He was far beyond healing. A sob wracked Stacy, and she pressed her palm over her mouth. Rowan passed her and went into the house to find Reginald. Ethan drifted behind Stacy and put a hand on her shoulder.

Esme did not seem to be aware of them despite Stacy's touch. Her eyes were clenched shut, and tears leaked down her cheeks. Stacy's thoughts whirled. *We should have been able to stop this. We should have guessed both estates would be attacked. This is too much.*

She let out another sob. Esme clutched Stacy's arm, murmuring something through her tears. Stacy didn't hear it. Ethan had walked off to examine the other bodies.

He came back as Rowan and Reginald emerged from the

house, and the three men spoke among themselves. Stacy glanced at Reginald, who was pale and grim, sorrow written on his face. He'd known Torin nearly his whole life, as had Esme. This house would never be the same.

Stacy caught some of Ethan's words. "Same as the Thorn estate. Wolves, witches, shifters, and vampires. Hired by the same people, no doubt. These attacks were planned to take place at the same time."

Stacy stood on wobbling legs, aware that Rowan was replying but unable to make out his words. She gazed at the forest beyond the house and the dark sky. She couldn't bear looking at Torin, knowing she would never hear him laugh or tease her again. These grounds would never look the same without his handiwork.

Ethan, Reginald, and Rowan were walking over to her, and Ethan was saying something. Stacy didn't hear it. Rage and sorrow swept through her like a tidal wave. She thought about her dragon form and shifted, then took off into the night.

"Torin meant a great deal to her. To all of us," Reginald murmured.

Ethan heard him, but he was watching Stacy vanish. If that was how she needed to grieve, so be it. His eyes went to the estate's cook Esme, who had not left Torin's side since she'd watched a werewolf tear his chest open.

"How did you kill them?" Rowan asked.

The butler's eyes were hollow. He took a long time to answer since the shock of his friend's death was still so new. "We set traps on the grounds we could trigger with magic. When I realized we were under attack, I set them off, and the blast killed most of them. I was too late for… I couldn't stop…" His voice trailed off.

Rowan told Reginald what had happened at the Thorn estate and their conclusions about who was behind it. "We will ask the Graytails to guard these grounds too. They want to see this place preserved as much as you do."

"Thank you," Reginald managed to get out.

Ethan walked toward the trees.

"Where are you going?" Rowan asked.

Ethan thought it was obvious. "To find Stacy."

He did not care about the cold wind or that he was tramping through the snow in shoes that would soak through. He did not care that he'd forgotten to take a coat or that it was the dead of night and he should have been in bed. All Ethan thought about was Stacy. He knew the rough direction she'd gone in and knew she would not fly forever. It wasn't good for her to be alone.

Emotions rattled through him. He hadn't known Torin well, but seeing a comrade and ally dead shook him. He'd told Stacy to rest before they formed a plan, but then this happened. They were out of time.

It was hard to believe that not long ago, Stacy had been a fledgling witch fighting battles in courts of law. Her world was far bigger now. He trekked down a narrow path that wound through the forest. It was quiet here, but not in an eerie or unsettling way. It was a deep, knowing quiet in which he felt like he was being watched by someone who would protect him. Despite Khan being gone, his presence lingered in the air.

Finally, Ethan came to a large clearing and halted. At least she was on the ground. Stacy lay in dragon form, wings at her sides. In the moonlight, the burnished gold-red of her scales looked paler. The edges of her wings glinted. Ethan approached, and she turned her massive head. Her eyes were gold, but they didn't hold the fierce determination they had when she was in human form. He saw sadness in them. It broke his heart.

Ethan had never imagined he would go to a dragon to

comfort her, much less that he would see a dragon's tear land on the snow. "Stacy."

She shifted, moving her wing so he could approach her. When he was close enough to place a hand on the side of her head, she brought her wing around him, shielding him from the wind. He gave her a faint smile. "You're always taking care of others. I know you needed to come here and just…feel."

Another tear fell on the snow. Stacy uttered what would have been a moan in human form. As a dragon, it was between a pained cry and a deep growl. Ethan stroked her scales. "I know why you haven't taken dragon form recently. When we saw the fae king, you told yourself the castle was too confined. Tonight, you probably told yourself it was too risky around your friends, but we can fight alongside a dragon, Stacy. We have done it before."

Her gold eyes met his. Ethan continued, "You only shift to fly somewhere, not to fight, but you will *need* to use your power. You were given this gift for a reason." His voice got firmer. "You're afraid because of what you saw in those creatures who came from Malabbra. You are not like that, Stacy, and you won't become like them."

Ethan's smile made another tear well in her eye. "We won't let you lose to the darkness. We'll be by your side to the bitter end."

Ethan remembered holding Luna's body as it went cold before he destroyed the tree and prevented the vampires from completing their ritual. Although they'd won, Ethan never looked back on that night without remembering the pain.

"Come back to me," he whispered, keeping the doubt and fear out of his voice. "The elves will arrive soon, and we can decide what to do together. Alerion can't hide whatever shit he has planned forever."

Stacy lifted her wing and nudged him with her muzzle. Ethan stepped back into the cold. A moment later, Stacy stood in human form, shivering. He wrapped his arms around her as sobs burst from her throat. Stacy buried her head in his neck, clutching his back. "I know," he murmured. He let her cry for several minutes, then drew back. "Let's go home."

Stacy wiped the tears from her cheeks, and a faint gold glimmer appeared in her eyes. That told Ethan she had thought of something. *I knew you would,* he thought.

CHAPTER EIGHTEEN

"I want to know what's taking them so long," Kiera murmured, the sound nearly like a growl. Her leg had not stopped bouncing since she and Amy sat at the kitchen table in the low light of a lamp. Amy was more than glad to avoid the fights, but it was difficult for Kiera to stand to the side while the others dealt with the infiltrators.

Amy had glanced outside before Miles allowed the ground to swallow the corpses. One werewolf had been injured, and Nox, the healing witch Amy had never heard speak, was tending to him.

"I want to know what went on at Khan's estate," Amy replied. It had also been attacked, and she had seen the horror on Stacy's face before she, Ethan, and Rowan left. Kiera had insisted she go with them, but Rowan had pleaded with her to stay behind. Kiera had been sullen since then. As Kiera's leg bounced, Amy drummed her fingers on her thigh, a dozen possibilities about what had happened coursing through her mind.

The back door opened, jolting her from her daze, and Miles trekked in, wearing a grim expression. "Now that that's done..."

"Where are the others? The coven witches, that is?" Kiera asked.

"Guarding at the back wall where the trespassers came in. We found holes in the wards. They managed to slip through without us realizing. Dem and Di are reinforcing the wards now. I should be with them, but I wanted to make sure everything was good in here."

"We're waiting," Amy replied. Ethan had come to check on them before they left, and though she was grateful for it, Amy and Kiera had been safe in the house.

Miles gave a curt nod and poured himself a glass of water. His expression shifted, emotions playing across his features. While Kiera was angry at herself for not being able to fight, Miles was beating himself up for letting enemies cross the wards he'd constructed and maintained since coming here.

No one should be blaming themselves for anything, Amy concluded, recalling the many times when she wished she'd been able to fight at their sides and didn't because she did not have magic. They all had their tasks. She knew that now but wished she could help the others see it as she did.

Kiera twisted in her seat, finally stilling her leg. "I saw them. Low-level assassins, weren't they?"

Miles nodded. "That's what Rowan and Stacy think. Rowan concluded that her remaining enemies in the underworld hired them."

Kiera's jaw tightened. She could have done away with more of those crooks if she hadn't been taken. "What do you think?" she asked Miles.

"The same thing. Those slimy scumbags want revenge on Stacy, and they would have figured out a way to get it."

"I agree, but it's more than that. This has my father written all over it."

Miles' brows furrowed. "The attack was messy. They couldn't beat us, and your father isn't a fool."

"No, he isn't," Kiera replied coolly. "He's all about distraction and trickery. They attacked here and at the Drakethorn estate at the same time for a reason. Whatever went on over there was done to weaken Stacy."

Amy's heart dropped when she thought about Reginald, Torin, and Esme. The Drakethorn estate was more secure in terms of magical protections, but far fewer people lived there. "Shit."

Kiera turned to Amy, remembering she was there. "That's how he's always done it. He moves in the shadows for a long time before striking. When he does strike…"

"He doesn't fucking miss," Miles finished. He drank the last of the water and set the glass on the counter. "He did this time."

Amy wished she was that confident. She sank back in the chair, thoughts wandering as Kiera and Miles continued their conversation. Miles described the mindless werewolves and bloodthirsty vampires and witches they'd fought. Amy didn't hear them; she was too involved in her thoughts.

The sound of the front door opening reached them. The trio in the kitchen waited until someone appeared. Ethan entered, looking harried and worn. "What happened?" Kiera immediately demanded. "Where is Stacy?"

Ethan nodded at the back door. "She went to the Guardian's Grove. She needs a minute."

Amy's heart thudded.

Ethan sat on the empty chair, his exhaustion evident in the slump of his soldiers. "Torin is dead." Miles muttered something under his breath. Kiera's jaw tightened again. Ethan told them what they'd found when they arrived at the estate and about Stacy shifting and flying away.

When he finished, Kiera shared a look with Miles and Amy. Had her father gotten Stacy's underworld enemies together?

"The elves will be coming soon, and Rowan is reaching out to the Graytails' Alpha," Ethan added. "Stacy... She's not doing well, but she's working on a plan."

"What did she tell you?" Amy asked.

"Nothing. I could just tell."

Amy stood. "Someone should—"

Ethan interrupted, "She wants to be alone. Said she needs to think."

About the plan. A way to come face to face with the fae king and defeat him. Amy sat again and sagged against the chair back. "How many more lives?" she murmured, thinking about Spencer, Luna, and Torin. "How many more before we're done?"

No one answered.

When Kiera found Rowan in his study, he wasn't sitting behind the desk. He stood at the window, arms folded, eyes fixed on the grounds below. She approached him silently and looked out at the Guardian's Grove, where Stacy had gone. Near the stone wall surrounding that portion of the estate, Demetrius and Diana were repairing and reinforcing the wards.

"We should have been better prepared," Rowan murmured.

"Don't start with that."

Rowan's eyes traveled to the Grove. "We have to be strong for Stacy. I can imagine what she is going through. If I lost one of you..."

Kiera did not need him to say her or Miles' name to understand what he meant. She reached for his hand and squeezed, remembering the times they'd thought they had lost one another.

Rowan continued, voice shaking, "I thought that after all those wars we fought hundreds of years ago, we would never have to do it again. Here we are, though, waiting for that fae piece of shit to wreck everything we have built."

Kiera agreed that the waiting was the hard part. It didn't help that the city's underworld had found a way to retaliate. Victor's former allies weren't finished taking out their vengeance on Stacy, but she couldn't fix her attention on them when Damien Hartwell and the fae king were out there.

Kiera leaned closer to Rowan, wanting to feel him while ignoring everything else. She'd made it out of that dungeon with her mind intact. Alerion had tried to shred it to out what she knew, but Stacy, Rowan, and Miles had come for her. "I hated sitting this out," she murmured and took his hand. "Nox is helping me heal still. I should be good to—"

Rowan spun to face her. "Don't rush your recovery for anyone's sake, Kiera. I'm sorry about earlier when I told you not to come with us. I can't bear the thought of…"

Kiera's grip on his hand tightened. "Stacy intends to face my father, and I won't let her do it alone. If anyone is prepared to face him, it is me. No one understands him better."

"She won't be alone-"

"I know that, Rowan, but I *have* to be there."

Rowan's mouth closed, and his shoulders slumped. "I know, Kiera." He had lost his parents in a war centuries ago, but he'd known them both and had a good childhood. Kiera had lost her mother when she was born, as Stacy had, and had only known a cruel father.

"Stacy can have the space she needs for the rest of tonight." She kissed his cheek, then let go of his hands.

"Where are you going?" he asked as she headed for the door.

Kiera flashed him a smile. "To sharpen my knives." She might not get a chance to stab Alerion through the heart, but she would be prepared.

Stacy was glad for the quiet.

In the Grove, all she heard was the soft wind blowing through the branches, brushing off the snow that lay there. She hadn't come in weeks and had forgotten how right it felt to stand here. She imagined her mother had come here whenever she felt overwhelmed.

Stacy dropped to her knees, not caring about the snow wetting her clothes. She was exhausted, but her mind kept turning over the recent events. The image of Torin's lifeless body would not soon leave her.

Her thoughts wheeled. *I lost someone I loved, but I am going to make them pay for taking his life. The underworld and the fae aren't the only ones against me now. Many of my allies think I killed their friends.*

How the hell was she supposed to fix all this?

"What if I can't do it?" she whispered, a tear dropping from her cheek. It was much smaller than her tears in dragon form. She hadn't cried as a dragon until tonight. She hadn't realized she could. Ethan had found her and done what he could to comfort her. Despite his efforts to be strong for her, his exhaustion and concern had not escaped her notice. Everyone was tired.

Stacy reached for the locket around her neck, comforted by the warmth emanating from it. The magic spread through her fingers, causing her skin to tingle, then passed into her arm and headed for her heart. It was as though Catherine stood behind her, resting a hand on her shoulder. *You can do this,* a voice that was not Stacy's asserted in her mind.

Perhaps she had imagined it, or maybe the Guardians had brought Catherine's spirit to her. Either way, Stacy clung to those words. She had to do this. The world was at risk, and all the magic in it, if Alerion was successful. He must be thrown out.

Stacy sensed rather than heard someone approaching. She turned her head enough to identify Kiera. The sidhe fae's face was solemn. "Stacy, you had better come to the gate. Someone is here."

Kiera did not look alarms. Was it the elves? Surely Elentya

could not have traveled so quickly. Perhaps it was other members of the Graytails.

She followed Kiera out of the Grove and around the house. The gate shone in the moonlight. The estate's guards, including Diana, Demetrius, and Miles, were wrestling with something between them on the ground. They were all crowded around whatever it was so that Stacy couldn't see it.

She hurried over. "What's going on? What is that?"

Miles looked focused as he sent his vines around the thrashing figure. The strain on Demetrius' and Diana's faces told Stacy that they'd been grappling with the thing for some time.

"I don't know why she bothered coming here," Kiera murmured from behind Stacy, arms folded under her breasts. "She must have a fucking death wish."

"She?" Stacy eyed the creature as Miles got her under control. The werewolves and the witches stepped back. Writhing in the grass, held down by Miles' vines, was a snake.

She was almost six feet long and had yellow scales and eyes. The snake writhed, then ceased, eyes closing. Stacy waited, already having a good idea of who had tried to wriggle in.

"We caught her coming under the gate and sensed it was more than a snake," Demetrius reported.

No sooner were the words out of his mouth than the snake shifted. The vines snapped, and a woman stood and dusted off her clothes. Viper gazed at Stacy, producing a feral grin. "Hello, Sweetheart," she crooned. "Did you miss me?"

CHAPTER NINETEEN

"You're lucky I don't cut off your head," Kiera hissed from Stacy's side.

Stacy was still reeling from the shock of seeing the snake shifter here. No one had seen Viper since she ran from the house she'd led the vampires into. *"What are you doing here?"*

Viper's smile widened despite Miles' vines cutting into her skin. "I have something to tell you, darling. You'll want to hear what I have to say."

"Be more specific, or you'll shed your skin for the last time," Kiera cut in. Stacy laid a warning hand on the sidhe fae's shoulder. Kiera simmered but snapped her mouth shut.

Viper kept her yellow eyes fastened upon Stacy. "It's about that foolish man Hartwell and his deal with the fae king. I'm sure you've figured some of it out, but I know more."

Stacy's heart dropped like a stone. "How the hell do you know about that?"

Viper rolled her eyes. "Please, sweetheart. I know everything. If you let me out of these fucking vines, we could have a real conversation."

Miles glanced at Stacy, one brow arched.

"Bring her inside, but put her in magic muffling chains so she can't shift," Stacy told him.

Viper opened her mouth to protest but after a glare from Kiera, she decided against it. Stacy narrowed her eyes. "You can explain why you're here, but we haven't forgotten how you betrayed us."

Viper only served herself, so her presence spoke volumes. She hadn't come because she was concerned about Stacy's welfare but because the fae king made her...afraid. Stacy realized Viper was afraid of what he would do if he were in power here.

Miles left the vines around Viper as they moved toward the house. One of the werewolves went ahead to ask Rowan for the chains. Stacy imagined how that conversation would go and smiled.

"What the hell is she doing here?" Ethan demanded as they entered the house. Amy lingered behind him, her cold eyes trailing over the vine-wrapped woman.

"That's what we're about to find out," Stacy replied. "Let's go to the library." The coven witches had retired for the remainder of the night, their tasks complete, so only Stacy, Ethan, Kiera, Miles, and Amy made their way to the library. Rowan strode in last, his eyes flashing with disdain as he beheld the shifter, muffling chains in hand.

Viper's lips curled into a sneer at the sight of the chains and the sigils glowing on them. Despite being unable to move or use her magic, she wasn't inclined to be pleasant. Miles removed the vines from each limb as Rowan slapped the chains around the shifter's wrists. "You've got balls coming here," Miles growled.

Rowan agreed. When he finished with the chains, Viper dropped into a chair by the fire, sighing. "Some hospitality you offer here. I expected better from you."

"Says the person who tried to kill me when I visited your place," Kiera replied, picking at her nails.

Viper scoffed. "You tried to kill me too."

"And yet, you're both alive," Rowan shot back.

Viper ignored him, her yellow gaze still pinned on Kiera. "I heard your daddy finally got hold of you. When I saw him last, he was looking for you. He asked if I knew where to find you."

Stacy expected Kiera to snap at the intruder, but Rowan surged toward the shifter. "You gave her away? You fucking—"

Miles and Ethan jumped up to restrain him.

"I didn't fucking *tell* him," Viper snapped, ignoring that the dryad had been close enough to snap her neck. "I told him this shit was none of my business and he could get fucked." She laughed hoarsely. "He didn't like that. If I hadn't shifted fast enough, he would have killed me. I barely escaped with my life."

Viper was too proud to admit something like that unless she was truly afraid. Stacy marveled at the thought of Viper and Alerion being in the same room, let alone having a conversation as she sat in the chair opposite Viper. "Start from the beginning. Where did you go after you abandoned your home and the vampires staying there?"

"It doesn't matter *where* I went," Viper returned coldly, turning her attention to Stacy.

Stacy sighed. "Look, we're all tired, so please don't be difficult. The faster we have this conversation, the better it will be for all of us."

Viper fidgeted. "I went north. I have many homes. I thought it was better to wait it out until the vampires were gone since when they came to me, they gave me no choice but to help them."

Stacy doubted that was true, but she allowed Viper to continue.

"When I realized you and your posse actually stood a chance against them, I took off."

"Instead of, you know, helping *us*?" Ethan inserted.

Viper shot him a smile. "You wish, darling."

Ethan's jaw tightened, but he didn't respond. Viper wanted a reaction, and he was determined not to give her one.

"What happened after you left?" Stacy asked. Miles and Ethan let go of Rowan, and he slid over to stand behind the chair Kiera occupied, chest heaving and hands balled into fists. Kiera was perfectly still in the chair, eyes never leaving Viper. She expected her to shift at any moment despite the chains.

Viper was a master of trickery, and Kiera had seen that in her father all her life, so she wasn't taking chances. Behind Rowan and Kiera, Amy leaned against the table, watching everything with a thoughtful expression. It occurred to Stacy then that this was the first time Amy had been around the snake shifter, though she'd heard plenty about Viper from the others.

"Damien Hartwell knew where one of my homes in the northern part of the state was. He came to visit me."

Damien had kept tabs on that matter too, then. He hadn't only been watching Stacy.

"He asked if I wanted to help him destroy you. Said he had many allies in the city's underworld willing to move when the time was right, and he wanted to offer me a position. Apparently, he's had connections in the underworld for years but didn't want to move until he saw what you did with Corbinelli and Hines.

"He'd come to see me in the city, so we were already acquainted. Months ago, he came looking for a witch and a bookshop." Viper eyed Ethan. "Don't worry. I didn't give you away. Not that it mattered since he doesn't have magic and wouldn't have found it anyway."

"How did he know about my shop?" Ethan demanded.

"Damien's mother was a witch," Stacy offered. "Maybe she knew about it."

Ethan seemed satisfied by that answer.

"Anyway, Hartwell was sniffing around like a dog, and I learned that he wanted to root out the criminals in the underworld. At first I thought he wanted criminals gone. That he was, shall we say, a noble FBI agent. I quickly realized it had nothing to do with organized crime. He simply hated *us*."

Viper motioned about the room, the chain around her wrist rattling. "For a long time, Hartwell thought the paranormals would destroy themselves." She laughed. "Then a dragon came onto the scene." Viper waved a dismissive hand. "He was vague about the whole thing, and I told him to go fuck himself unless he could make me an offer that involved…physical compensation."

Ethan cringed.

The snake shifter rolled her eyes. "I wasn't inviting Hartwell into my bed. You know I like my treasures. He simply didn't want to go treasure hunting."

Stacy didn't want to know what that meant, but she remembered that in the past, Ethan had brought the shifter odd gifts in exchange for arcane books.

"I considered working with him if he offered me a better deal, but then I found out about the fae, and Damien realized he had to sweeten the pot with information." Viper drummed her long black nails on the arm of the chair. "He told me he'd found a way to pierce the veil into the fae world and bring them through. He'd been studying how to do that for years. Apparently, Damien has had a fascination with Malabbra and dragons his whole life."

Stacy's breath caught. "Why?"

Viper shrugged. "Something about his mother being a witch who'd been seduced by dark magic. He was intrigued by that and told me she had many books about that dark world that he read after she died."

Stacy and Ethan shared a look. So, there *was* more information out there. Stacy wished she had taken a better look at the shelves at the Hartwell house.

Viper continued. "Hartwell hates having paranormals in high places and wants them destroyed. He considers all of us terrorists."

"He told you that?" Ethan asked, one brow raised.

Viper chuckled. "Of course not. I pried my way into his mind and saw the thoughts he didn't say out loud. He has allies in the FBI—other rogue agents who are working with a larger conspiracy across the world to bring paranormals down a notch or two." Her eyes roved over Stacy. "Especially ones with power and money."

"And Damien thinks that bringing in one of the most powerful paranormals, the fae king, will accomplish that," Kiera inserted.

"Damien is a fool," Viper replied. "He baited the fae king into coming to our world, promising its magic. Somehow, he learned that the fae world was dying."

A flicker of sorrow went through Kiera's eyes, vanishing almost as quickly as it had appeared.

"For some reason, Damien believes he can defeat the fae king after he deals with you dragons." Viper scoffed, shaking her head. "Damien did his research on the dark world, but he doesn't know shit about the fae."

Unless Damien knew something else, Stacy thought. Something he found out after his mother's death in her books. Perhaps Viper hadn't scoured his mind thoroughly. What could it be?

"I don't want to live in a world where that fae piece of shit rules us," Viper continued. "I will work with whoever I have to so that doesn't happen."

Ethan snorted. "For once, we agree, Viper." Her answering sweet smile held a touch of poison, and Ethan glowered. "You have only ever worried about yourself. How can we know you won't betray us again?"

Viper leaned forward, chains rattling. "I've put my ass on the line by coming here and telling you this."

"That doesn't mean you won't betray us when there's a war and it's easier for you to run and hide or sell us out to save yourself," Ethan retorted. "You've always chosen the easy way out."

Viper's yellow eyes glowed. "You have no fucking idea what I've been through."

Ethan opened his mouth to respond, then decided against it.

Stacy spoke up. "You will be our guest until we know more, Viper, and you will remain in those chains." She nodded at Miles. "Take her to the safe room and seal it. Post guards outside."

Miles nodded. Viper rolled her eyes as he hauled her up from the seat. "Such hospitality."

"We'll send food and water down," Stacy added. Viper ran her eyes over Stacy from head to foot, then lifted her chin. After Viper and Miles had left the room, everyone turned to their leader.

"We can't trust her," Ethan stated.

"Thanks, Captain-fucking-Obvious," Kiera muttered.

"I think you need to be in bed," Ethan retorted. "Someone's grumpy."

They all were.

"She's given us helpful information," Rowan inserted before Kiera could reply to Ethan's remark. "Assuming she isn't lying, Damien and the fae king have aligned and are using the murdered magicals and Stacy's current unpopularity in the underworld to incite something against her. Flames they plan to fan until we're all engulfed."

"Then what?" Ethan asked. "They want to get the dragons out of the way and make the world theirs?"

Kiera jumped in. "My father will do away with Damien and anyone else involved in this world conspiracy, then take the magic he wants out of Earth. Damien wants to kill my father and the rest of us. I agree with Viper. Damien is stupid."

"Or he knows something." Amy mused. She hadn't said a word since she entered the room.

All eyes went to her, but Stacy said, "I was thinking the same thing. We need to find out what Damien discovered about the dark world. Maybe it could help us defeat Alerion."

"I don't see how we're supposed to do that," Rowan protested.

"I need to see Damien again," Stacy replied and stood.

"He's on the run," Ethan reminded her. "The FBI is after him."

"Then *we* need to catch him. I am forming a plan, but I need more time."

"We're out of that," Kiera inserted.

Stacy met her gaze. "I know." The events of the night came crashing back down upon her, and the names of the dead rattled through her mind.

She thought about what Viper had said about Damien not making a better offer and something sparked in her brain. Amy observed the change in Stacy's expression. "What are you thinking?"

Stacy smiled despite her sorrow. "I'm going to make Damien Hartwell an offer he can't refuse." She turned to Rowan. "First, call Agent Davos and tell her to be ready. I'm about to deliver his traitorous ass to her on a silver platter."

CHAPTER TWENTY

Stacy closed her eyes as a cold breeze caressed her face.

Snow was softly falling, and she wrapped her coat around her tighter. Her cheeks and the tips of her ears were red, but she wanted to be in the Grove for this.

She heard footsteps on the snow-covered path behind her, followed by Hartwell's taunt. "You finally came to your senses."

Stacy opened her eyes and enjoyed the way the afternoon sunlight played on the white puffs on the branches. She turned to see Damien standing at the Grove's entrance, hands stuffed into the deep pockets of his coat. His sharp gaze roved around the space between the trees, then returned to her. He studied her with unashamed intensity as if all the pieces in his plan were falling into place.

Stacy had left him a voicemail offering to do whatever he wanted as long as he didn't sell her out to the FBI. He wouldn't refuse to have her under his control.

Damien's quick arrival told her he had returned to this area beforehand, probably to seek Alerion's protection in New York City's underworld.

"My home was attacked last night," Stacy began. She watched

for a reaction, but his face was unreadable. "By people who believed I murdered magicals. I didn't do it, but I see why you think I did. I need legal protection, and I know you can offer it. I will do what I must to help you with your *plans*, whatever they are. We *are* more similar than I realized."

She hated saying the words, but they produced the response she'd expected and hoped for.

Damien smiled. "I came back to the area because I thought you might see sense after our last meeting. You need help beyond what your magical friends can provide. I'm glad you now understand that."

Stacy felt like punching his lights out.

Damien tilted his head. "Why are we out in the cold? Your maid said you wanted to meet here."

Stacy tried not to bristle since Kiera was not a maid, but she pasted on a smile and told him the truth. "This spot is special to me because it is where my mother came when she was overwhelmed by outside matters."

She drifted closer to him as snow flecked her unbound auburn hair. "After we met for the first time, I found out your mother went mad and died in the middle of the forest and that some suspected your father of murdering her." She spoke softly, but her words and eyes probed him.

Damien shifted his weight, and his voice turned cold. "What does that have to do with anything?"

"I know the truth," Stacy murmured. "She went mad because of her magic, didn't she?"

"How did you know that?" he snapped.

Stacy shrugged. "I noticed the books in your house." That was a lie, but she didn't want to reveal that Viper had come to them until he told her what she needed to know.

Damien narrowed his eyes, then sighed. "After she died, I wanted to find out what had caused her madness. She had these books hidden in a trunk. I'd always been curious about them and finally worked up the courage to read them after she was gone. I wish I had done so before. Maybe I..." He swallowed, his gaze distant. It was the first sincere emotion Stacy saw on his face. "Maybe I could have stopped it before she died, or I used to think so. I'm now convinced that nothing could have prevented it."

"What magic did she have?" Stacy prodded.

Damien fixed her with a dark stare. "Magic from another world where evil things breed. Her father was a warlock from that world, so she had dark magic in her veins from the day she was born."

Stacy examined him. "The dragons came from that world too, so we also have darkness in our veins."

"Yes," he agreed tightly.

Stacy tilted her head. "It's unlike an FBI agent to take me up on my offer. If I *were* a murderer and a terrorist, you would hand me over the first chance you got, but you want to use me as a means to your ends. I don't think you're with the FBI anymore."

Damien's face froze, then a smile appeared on his lips. "Nice try, Stacy."

She wasn't done yet. She dropped the soft tone. "You came to meet me at my father's estate to learn enough to kill me. Maybe not right then, but you intended to set the stage. You want all creatures, including dragons, who originated from the dark place to die because you believe we're all poisoned by that magic."

Damien bristled. "Dragons should never be in power. They all go mad!"

Stacy shook her head. "Anyone can go mad from power. I know of several incidents where *you* did hateful things to paranormals of all kinds. Your record is...well, complicated. I wonder if your power went to your head." Amy had unearthed things that should have gotten Damien kicked out of the FBI a long time ago, but he'd covered his tracks well, so it had taken her a good deal of time to find anything of substance.

"I'm not going to trial, Damien, but you are," she finished.

He froze. "What the fuck does that mean? Why did you bring me here? You tricked me!"

"You tricked me first," she replied, folding her arms. "After we finish this conversation, I will take you inside. A couple of old friends want to see you, though I don't think they consider themselves friends anymore."

Damien paled, and his voice shook. "Wh-what are you talking about?"

"I think you and Agent Davos and Agent Taylor are long overdue for a catch-up." She allowed a glimmer of gold into her green eyes, a hint that a dragon lived beneath her human skin, and she was done keeping it contained.

"I don't know what they told you, but it's all a lie!" Damien snarled. He started to stomp away, but Stacy's words halted him.

"There's no use in running. My guards are all over this estate. You won't be leaving except with Agent Davos and Agent Taylor." She shrugged as he turned back, hate burning in his eyes. "Go for it. I'd like to watch you try." If his former colleagues wanted to shoot his traitorous ass, they could for all she cared, but more was at stake here, and they needed Damien to expose it. The FBI could handle the investigation of the anti-paranormal conspiracy while Stacy dealt with Alerion.

She registered that he'd taken his right hand out of his pocket, but she did not see the gun before he fired at her head. A blaze of energy leapt up around her. The bullet struck with the magical shield and fell to the ground.

Damien gaped. "What—"

She didn't have time to respond before two people stepped out of the trees. Demetrius emerged from the left, his hard eyes tracking Damien's every move. Stacy realized he'd flung up the shield.

Diana slipped from the trees behind Damien and snatched the gun out of his hands, then prodded him with a knife. "We're done with these outdoor games," she crooned.

Demetrius kept the shield around Stacy as she gave Damien a bitter smile. "Former Agent Hartwell, these good people are members of my coven. Demetrius and Diana, please take this man inside."

"With great pleasure," Diana purred.

"One more thing," Stacy called as they turned to the Grove's exit. Damien had turned purple with rage, but desperation dancing in his eyes. "You might suffer less from those you betrayed if you tell me what you know about the fae king."

"I don't know what you're talking ab—" Damien sputtered.

She cut him off. "Oh, please. I know you're part of the reason Alerion is here." Recognition at the name flashed through his eyes; it was all the evidence Stacy needed. She approached him, leaving only a few inches left between their faces. The magic shield sizzled in the air between them. She adopted the soft tone she'd used when he arrived. "You know how to weaken the fae king. Tell me."

Stacy stood in the library alone, her eyes and fingers trailing over Ethan's notes on Malabbra. Agent Davos and Agent Taylor had taken a furious Damien away, thanking Stacy for her help and promising their aid in the future. Damien's ranting and raving still echoed in the hallway.

Stacy had retreated here to think everything over. Except for the crackle of flames in the hearth, the room was silent. She scanned the draconic runes Ethan had shown her before, and her mind went back to her mother. Catherine and Khan had drawn symbols of dragon origin around the estate to protect the magic this place had been built upon. One of the noblest witches for generations, Catherine had thought highly of dragon magic. She had married a dragon, after all.

Stacy's smile faded as she considered all the things she still didn't know about her mother, namely, how she had died. Khan had only told her that she had died of an ailment shortly after Stacy's birth. Was there more to it than that, and Khan had simply found it too painful to speak about? Her father had always tried to protect her, which was why he hadn't revealed her true nature until earlier this year. It was possible that he hadn't yet told her the full truth of her mother's death, no matter how much Stacy hoped he had.

Her thoughts were disrupted by a conversation beyond the door and the entrance of Kiera and Amy. The latter spoke. "Queen Elentya and some of her court have arrived, as well as the Graytails' Alpha. They await you out front and are eager to see you."

Stacy glanced out the window. The sun was close to setting, and its blood-orange rays danced over the wooden floorboards. She returned her attention to Kiera. "Have them meet me in here so we can speak privately."

Stacy braced herself and smoothed the front of her pants, then pushed her hair behind her ears. It had been months since she had seen either leader, and she had not been in the room with both at the same time.

"Are you pissing yourself?" Amy whispered. "I am."

Stacy cast her a wry smile. "I think we're going to make it." Elentya and the Alpha could be intimidating, but they were good women.

They entered together, with Kiera trailing behind them. Elentya was as tall and regal as Stacy remembered, her dark skin set off by her green clothing. She was dressed in human attire today: an evergreen sweater and flowing black pants. The gold jewelry adorning her ears, neck, and hair indicated her royal status, and she hadn't bothered to glamour her perfect features and pointed ears.

The broad-shouldered woman beside her was shorter but no less intimidating. Sleek silver hair framed the Alpha wolf's ice-blue eyes, and a fang-shaped pendant hung around her neck. She had opted to wear warm wool clothes and a dark blue and silver robe. Stacy had never learned the Alpha's name. She was simply known as "the Alpha" to those outside her pack.

"Thank you both for coming and for your continued support," Stacy began. "I'm sure Rowan and Miles caught you both up on recent events if you hadn't already heard."

"They did, as did the wolves who have been guarding your estate," the Alpha replied, her voice as crisp as the November wind. "Moreover, I bring news. I know that both your estates were attacked last night. So were our lands."

Stacy's heart sank. "What happened?"

"Fucking hell," Amy muttered.

"Some of the patrolling wolves were taken by surprise. Three are injured, but we believe they will recover." The Alpha's eyes glinted. "I always believed there was a threat, but I am far more interested in seeing it removed now."

Elentya spoke next. "Rowan has been in touch these past several weeks and more often in recent days. You are walking through a difficult time, both of you." She directed this last bit at both Stacy and the Alpha. "My land was attacked when the vampires attempted their ritual, so I understand your plight. You helped me, Ms. Drakethorn, and I haven't forgotten that. You have my allegiance."

She had to give them the full scope of the problem. If either backed out, she'd be disappointed, but she would understand. "A very difficult time is ahead of us, which is why I wanted to speak to you both. I have a plan, but I can't do anything without your help."

Stacy motioned to the chairs and sofas, and the women made themselves comfortable. She began with what had happened earlier that day, then told them that former Agent Hartwell was out of the picture for now and they needed to deal with Alerion before he raised the whole underworld against her.

"Against *us*," Stacy corrected. "He is coming after me for now, but once I'm gone—"

"We are well aware of what he plans to do when you are gone," the Alpha interrupted. "Elentya and I govern lands ripe with magic that someone like him will covet. We aren't foolish enough to think he won't be at our throats as soon as he can."

"The fae have always had a tendency toward the extreme," Elentya added. "At least, in my experience." Her sharp eyes roved to Kiera, who stood by the window.

Kiera shrugged. "I don't take any offense. I agree to an extent. Not all fae, but many from my homeworld are like him. We were raised in that environment. If you aren't cutthroat from the time you can speak and can't wield weapons and magic by the time you can run, you're as good as dead."

There was a heavy silence before the Alpha turned to Stacy. "If we can defeat Alerion, that will be good, but what about your other enemies?"

"We will deal with the underworld criminals when the time comes. They won't have a leg to stand on after I'm through with the fae king."

"I've heard about his cruelty and what he did to those magicals. How can we hope to defeat him?" the Alpha asked.

Stacy heard the concern in her voice. The Graytails never showed fear, but they were realistic and had been through hell at the hands of Victor Corbinelli. Alerion would be worse.

"I have a plan, as I said." Stacy gestured for Kiera to come forward. "Kiera was the bait, both when Damien got her father to come to this world and when Alerion framed me for murder. She has agreed to be the bait again."

"Except this time, I will have a say in the matter," Kiera interjected drily.

"I plan to lure the fae king to my father's estate and face him there. I need you both to fight beside me if I am to have any hope of defeating him."

"Of course I will fight at your side!" Elentya exclaimed.

"After everything you have done for our people and the proximity of your lands, I will do the same," the Alpha agreed.

Stacy flashed a smile. "They want to kill a dragon? They can try."

Elentya matched her smile and straightened, clasping her hands together. "This is unfolding exactly as I thought it would. The prophecy about you is coming to fruition."

Stacy's expression shifted to puzzlement. Kiera and Amy stilled.

"What prophecy?" Amy asked.

"The one we learned about from Adrian before the whole deal with the vampires," Kiera answered.

Stacy had written it off, but she remembered that Elentya and the elves had heard it before, and that was the reason Elentya had wanted to meet her. Gods, it felt like ages since she'd first laid eyes on the elf queen, but less than a year had passed.

Elentya closed her eyes. "I know the words as if they were written on my heart.

"Dark pestilence abounds
Of strife, war, and blood it sounds
On wings of gold comes our vindication,
Born of witch and serpent both.
Magic and might as condemnation
Shall strike with sword and breath of flame
That which stands with death in hand
Through a powerful, inherited name."

The prophecy was ancient, so Stacy didn't think it had anything to do with her. Still, some of those words hit home. "How did your people hear of it? Have the elves have always known about it?"

The elf queen shook her head, tight braids swaying around her face. "I heard it for the first time shortly before you were born."

Amy's brows knitted. "How?"

"Someone told me." The queen spoke as if it were the obvious answer.

Someone had told Elentya, but they'd found out about it from a book kept deep underground by an elusive sidhe librarian.

"Who?" Kiera demanded impatiently.

Stacy knew the answer from the elf queen's expression.

Elentya's eyes locked with Stacy's. "Catherine Thorn."

CHAPTER TWENTY-ONE

It was cold and dark outside, but Stacy ignored the external conditions as she stepped through the back door into the barren garden. Reginald Blackguard stood ahead, facing the grounds and the forest stretching beyond. Stacy could imagine what plagued his mind: the fear that more friends would die if they were attacked again.

They would be—on her terms.

Rowan was waiting for Stacy in front of the house. He had told her to take all the time she needed. For her plan to work, she needed Reginald's help. When she reached his side, he turned, a tear drifting down his cheek.

He wiped it away and summoned a faint smile to his lips. "Good evening, Miss Anastasia."

Stacy looped her arm through his. "Don't bother with protocol, Regi. We've been through so much." Her heart ached to be here since Esme was mourning, Reginald's heart was broken, and Torin...

Stacy swallowed. *I'll never hear his joyous laughter again.*

Reginald patted her hand. "It's too cold out here. You should be inside."

"I could say the same about you." She tugged him onward. "Let's walk. It will keep our feet from freezing, and I need to tell you what has happened." It had stopped snowing, and most of what remained had melted, thanks to the sun being out all day. Out here, only the light of lamps and candles flooding through the windows illuminated their path.

Stacy matched Reginald's slower gait as they passed what would be blooming rose bushes in a few months. Some were still alive by the windows, panes and petals kissed by frost. The wind was cold enough to turn Stacy's cheeks and nose red, but she did not suggest that they go inside. She told Reginald about Viper's visit that morning and how she had dealt with Damien later. She spoke of Elentya's and the Alpha's dedication to helping her, and that she had a plan.

"I need your help, Regi. Please tell me about how the magic on this place works. Where the ley lines are and where the magic is the strongest. I have some idea, but you know the grounds better."

"Whatever you need." They halted, and he pointed outward. "The ley lines run diagonally across the grounds toward the center here." A faint smile came to his lips. "See that spot where your father normally shifts?"

Stacy nodded.

"Three of the lines intersect there, so it has the most power."

"Thank you, Regi."

"Remember, the magic is fickle. The lines sometimes…well, they move."

"Move?" Stacy echoed.

Reginald nodded. "It's not as though they grow legs and run off, but the magic flows like small rivers deep within the earth, and sometimes, those rivers change course. I can feel them shifting even now. They ebb and flow, always changing. That is why magic is so difficult to control."

Stacy imagined Alerion infiltrating the earth and taking that rich, warm magic. He wouldn't be able to, though, not without bringing a considerable amount of dark magic against it. This land and its ley lines were far older than her father, and they could not easily be removed.

Stacy swallowed. "Have you heard from my father?"

Reginald shook his head. "I have tried every way I know to reach him. I am certain you have done the same."

She nodded. "I have." She paused. "Regi, Elentya brought up a prophecy she heard from my mother before I was born. I heard it weeks ago, but I didn't give it much thought. We had so much going on."

Reginald halted and turned to meet Stacy's gaze. "I know the prophecy you speak of. Your mother told me too. Told me that..." He swallowed. "That *you* were the best chance."

"For what?"

Reginald's eyes held sorrow, but he wrapped his arm around her shoulders and resumed walking. "I have something to tell you, Anastasia. I have always wanted to, but my devotion was first and foremost to your father, who commanded me not to speak of your mother's death while he was in this house. I suppose now that he is away, and given the recent circumstances, I had better tell you."

Stacy's interest was piqued.

"Your father does not like keeping secrets from you," Reginald added. "This was simply too painful for him to speak of, and he didn't want us to either."

Us, as in Esme and Torin. They all knew whatever he was about to tell her.

"I heard Damien Hartwell's story when he came here, and now you tell me his witch mother died of a sickness from dark magic." Reginald's voice was grim.

"Yes. Go on."

"Mr. Hartwell was right when he said you and he had much in common. Your mother also died from the magic in the dark world."

Stacy halted and peered at Reginald's face. "What are you saying?"

Reginald's voice quavered. "It took over her mind, and instead of succumbing to madness…she, well, she wasn't in pain when she died. She went with all the peace one could hope for, comfortable and loved. You should know that."

An ache exploded in Stacy's chest. "That's not possible. My mother was a witch with no ties to the dark world. How could that have happened?"

Reginald shuddered. "You happened, Anastasia."

She came to a sickening realization and blew out a breath. "I am half-dragon, so the magic of that dark world is in my blood. Enough to…to…" She broke off.

Reginald's arm tightened. "She gave birth to you without complications, but the darkness from your magic remained inside her. That darkness is diminished because—"

"There isn't much left. That darkness leached into my mother and it…it killed her, didn't it?" Stacy didn't bother suppressing the tears that welled in her eyes.

Reginald gave a solemn nod.

It felt like someone had slid a knife into Stacy's gut. Guilt and sorrow rose, joining a torrent of emotions pounding in her heart.

"Your father blamed himself. He probably still does. He never wanted you to know that same feeling of guilt, so he never told you the truth."

Too late.

Stacy's voice shook. "Why tell me now?"

"You should know everything with the fae king coming. You are *good*, Stacy, and you will not be overtaken by darkness. You will rise above it. Vanquish it."

It was the first time Reginald had called her "Stacy" instead of "Anastasia." The ache in her throat made it difficult to force words to her tongue. "M-my mother. Did she know?"

Again, Reginald nodded. "When she discovered she was pregnant, she knew she might die. She hoped the darkness in your magic would pass to her since she loved your father dearly and refused to end your life. She wanted to give him a child who shared his legacy so the Drake line would continue. She didn't want him to be the last dragon since someone of his might and power would one day be needed. That dragon would possess the goodness of her magic and character as well."

A tear rolled down Stacy's cheek.

Reginald continued, his voice thick with emotion. "Knowing she might die, she shaped your legacy both as his heir and her daughter. She wanted you to know your heritage fully." Reginald moved Stacy's auburn hair and brushed the tree mark on her neck. The locket pulsed with warmth.

"Despite knowing what having you might do to her, Catherine loved you more than anything in the world."

Stacy squeezed her eyes shut, unable to stop her tears. This was too much.

Reginald's voice was her sole comfort. "As for the elves, your mother went to them before you were born. Catherine was friends with Elentya's mother, the former queen of the elves. Elentya's mother was near death when Catherine went to her, and since Elentya would soon become their queen, she shared the prophecy.

"She knew Khan would become a shell of his former self after she was gone, and she wanted to ensure that others would give you the strength to act. Oh, Khan would fight for you and protect you, but your mother foresaw your need for allies. That is why she left you the Thorn estate and went to the elves."

Reginald drew another breath. "She told Elentya and her

court the prophecy so that when you were older and encountered the dark elements, they would know who you were and help you."

"This mark on my neck," Stacy got out. "It is the symbol of my mother's coven, but it is also on the elven gate on Elentya's land."

Reginald's expression remained somber. "Your mother requested it be put there as a sign of your coming to save their people and their land." A smile graced his lips. "That part of her prophecy has already come to pass."

They neared a stone bench, and, unable to stand any longer, Stacy sank onto it. Reginald did the same. "The symbol on that gate was also a sign that your mother was always there for you, guiding your steps. Catherine knew about your legacy, both sides of it, and meant for you to defeat the darkness that came your way."

Stacy wished her father was here. She finally understood why their relationship had been so complicated. Khan had carried this secret in his heart, not wanting her to share his sorrow and guilt.

"Before you were born, your mother came to me," Reginald went on. His voice dropped to a whisper, not because he thought they would be overheard but because he did not want it to break. "She made me promise to protect you and help your father see that you were meant for greatness and he should not be afraid of showing you your power."

"When I came back in the spring, you weren't here," Stacy recalled.

"I wasn't, but before I went, I told your father he must face the truth and share your true legacy with you."

Reginald had always had her best interests at heart. He released a soft laugh. "Esme and Torin told your father the same thing and made him promise to bring you back. We missed you more than we could say. So did Khan."

He didn't say "Lord Drakethorn," which surprised Stacy.

She gripped his hand. "Thank you for telling me, Regi. I see things more clearly now. That was what I needed to finish this." Stacy wiped her tears away and smiled. "I will make my mother's sacrifice count.

"It already does," Reginald replied as his tears fell. "Your mere existence is enough, Anastasia. It always has been."

CHAPTER TWENTY-TWO

It was quiet here.

Kiera pushed up her sleeve and angled the sleek dagger toward her arm, brows knitted in concentration. *You've felt worse pain than this,* she reminded herself. Yesterday, when Stacy told her what she had in mind, Kiera realized she had to find a way to lure her father onto the grounds.

"There is a kind of fae ritual magic I have not used on this world," she'd confessed in the dim, quiet confines of the library. Kiera had waited until she had Stacy alone, knowing that Rowan would disapprove of using dark magic despite it being the only way. "It is only effective between blood relatives. They're called summoning sigils. My father used them whenever he wanted to call upon me or my brothers and sisters."

Stacy had agreed to her proposal since Kiera thought it would work and was the best approach. Now the sidhe fae stood on the grounds, feeling the hum of magic within the earth. The ley lines ran so deep here that she hardly felt their presence. It would take considerable effort to plunge into that magic and use it.

She clenched her jaw, and then crimson fluid bubbled onto her skin as, one by one, Kiera carved two summoning sigils, one to indicate where she was and one to call him to her. She spoke the incantation through her pain.

Kiera closed her eyes, aware of the hot blood and the cold wind. The dagger at her side dripped her blood.

She felt his presence before he spoke, but she did not open her eyes until he said, "You have never summoned me before, daughter. You must have something to say." He sounded irritated, as if she had pulled him away in the middle of a task.

He stood before her, wearing the same gold robe and crown she'd last seen him in. This time, she wasn't in chains or on her knees. Kiera lifted her chin. "It worked."

The king inclined his head. "What do you want?" His voice almost sounded kind, but Kiera knew better than to give in to his tricks.

"You're done here in this world. We can send you back, or, if you prefer, we can send you to your death."

He laughed. "'We?'" He stepped closer, drenching her in his sickening dark magic. Kiera grasped for the threads of warmth in her magic, willing it to stave off the waves around him.

"We've already dealt with Damien Hartwell," was her response.

Alerion laughed again. The sound skittered over her bones like snow blowing down a tree branch. "Then you did me a favor. I didn't need him anymore." His lips curled in a sneer. "You cannot hope to defeat me, Lia. My plan is already in motion."

She hated hearing that name, but she ignored it since the last thing her father needed was a reaction. "I know what you are," she offered instead.

A shadow passed through her father's eyes, but he seemed curious.

"Damien found out, but you already know that," she continued. "Stacy convinced him to tell her."

"He lied," Alerion snapped.

Kiera brushed a snowflake off her cloaked shoulder. "We'll

have to see then, won't we? I know what you are, and I know that you came from the dark world."

Alerion opened his mouth to respond, but Kiera's attention went to the edge of the forest and the Drakethorn estate beyond. A rallying cry arose, but it did not come from anyone Kiera knew. The next moment, magic slammed into her—the fae warriors Alerion had brought with him.

Her shadows answered of their own accord, rising to curl around her. Her father wore a wicked smile. "Perhaps I do come from Malabbra and the magic of that world flows through my veins. If it flows through mine, it also flows through yours." He nodded at her shadows, then vanished.

There were more warriors than Ethan expected.

First came the blast of magic. With Reginald's guidance, they'd dismissed the wards surrounding the Drakethorn estate before the sun set.

Ethan steadied himself, looking steely and grim when the warriors appeared. They emerged from thin air, brandishing curved swords and clad in shimmering gold armor and flowing capes. At first, he wondered if he had stumbled into their world. Their mere presence made him feel as though he were no longer anywhere he knew.

To Ethan's left stood Rowan, and to Rowan's left was Miles. Behind Miles were the Graytails' Alpha and her warriors, some snarling and others pawing at the ground, barely restraining themselves from launching. They waited for Miles' signal.

Behind Rowan were the elves, led by their queen. Elentya carried a bow and a quiver of arrows, all singing the song of elven magic—weapons forged by her mighty ancestors in the woodlands.

Behind Ethan stood the coven. Demetrius and Diana were

prepared to fling up shields. Emile followed them, and Nox was wavering in the shadows, ready to heal those who were injured.

The fae passed the tree line and approached the gate. Ethan turned to Rowan, and the dryad nodded. They took off as a single force: Ethan and the coven, Rowan and the twelve elves, and Miles and the eight werewolves. They were few compared to the dozens of fae warriors surging through the gate, but they only had to fend off these trespassers long enough to give Stacy and Kiera the time they needed.

Ethan tore down the hill with Demetrius' shield of magic bubbling around him. He summoned his magic and cast it at the gate as the fae entered. His spell touched the ground, and the unfortunate fae warrior who stepped foot there a second later was caught in the explosion.

Emile cast the same runes, and the twins flung defensive magic, but the fae batted away the strikes with their swords, shields, and magic. A wall of white-hot energy shot into the air, and Ethan skidded to a halt. Past him, the elves under Rowan's and Elentya's lead also stopped, and the wolves howled at the obstacle.

"Now!" Rowan called as he, Ethan, the witches, and Miles gathered their magic, then threw it at the fae's wall in unison. Their magic blasted through the wall, and the warriors crashed into the gate.

Ethan had wanted to remain by the house and set off the traps Reginald had used when the estate was last attacked, but the butler had revealed the traps could be reset in time to fend off these warriors, and some of the fae were strong enough to survive them. So here they were, Ethan thought, throwing every ounce of their power at these otherworldly warriors.

The elves nocked their arrows and fired. Before the forces crashed into one another, Elentya and her warriors injured many. She strode at Rowan's side, shooting one arrow after another. Rowan leapt toward the horde, slashing his ax through their armor.

The thuds and clanks of swords and axes and knives colliding filled Ethan's ears, but he continued casting runes at places Emile had not. On his right, the snarling wolves careened down the hill, dodging the flying magic and launching at the fae.

One large silver and blue wolf bristling with the thirst to kill leapt into the fray, finding throats and guts and limbs to tear. Damn, their Alpha was good. Ethan shouldn't have expected anything less.

Kiera and Stacy were absent, and Amy was at the Thorn estate with Reginald and Esme. Ethan thought they had a chance. The fae were more numerous, but they had not expected such a coordinated defense.

The ground shook when the groups collided, and the magic nearly blinded attackers and defenders alike. *Keep going,* Ethan told himself despite the blood coating his clothes and the sweat pouring down his body. He strained to pull more magic from the well within, but he was losing focus and strength.

A loud roar almost deafened him. His heart lurched and he spun, knowing Demetrius' shield would stay intact. A winged creature with a long, sweeping tail and gleaming talons soared into the night sky. The dragon's scales glowed like fire in the starlight.

Ethan smiled, but then it faded. He did not recognize this dragon.

Stacy's scales were red as well as gold, and this dragon was larger than her. Khan? It couldn't be. Khan was called the Red Dragon for a reason. Ethan experienced a rush of dread and horror. That wasn't just a dragon. It was a fae.

Alerion.

"He's like you," Damien answered coldly.

Stacy folded her arms while Diana raised a brow. Demetrius stood beside her, as still as a statue, his eyes not leaving Damien despite his sister holding her knife to his back. "What do you mean?" Stacy asked.

Damien's eyes flashed. "Isn't it fucking obvious? He's a *dragon*. Alerion, the high fae king, came from Malabbra, though no one in the fae world knows since he hid that. Burned any books that held the secret and did the same to people. His mother was a dragon, but his father was fae. He inherited his father's looks but has always been able to shift."

Stacy laughed. "You're telling me that even though a whole world of fae is unaware their king is a dragon, *you* know? I find that hard to believe."

"Then don't," Damien snapped. "But that's the truth."

She stepped closer, eyes flashing gold. "How the fuck do you know?"

"My mother stole the knowledge from my grandfather, a warlock who'd slipped through a crack from Malabbra into our world. He said that something evil had happened in that world, and a creature that was half-dragon and half-fae had been responsible."

Stacy shivered.

Damien went on, ire rising. "He didn't explain what happened, but he drew pictures. The dead filled the cities and wastelands. Somehow, my grandfather escaped, and my mother stole his books where he'd written the account in the old language of dark magic. That was how she became tainted. She spent too much time reading his damn books, and they drove her mad."

Ethan had told her about magical tomes where, by opening them, one's mind was transported to the time and place of the events described within. Spend enough time in those books, and you would think you were there. No wonder Damien's mother had gone mad.

"After I found out about Alerion, I wanted to meet him," Damien concluded. "If he could do such disastrous things there, he could come here and do the same thing."

"How did you do it?"

"I've been studying magic for years," Damien replied bitterly. "My mother's books told me about a veil and a place on my estate where someone could access other worlds. She had gone there to speak to her dead father, so I went at the time she had. I got fucking lucky was what happened. I saw the fae king beyond the veil, and I saw what he'd done to his world. I thought of a plan, and I told him what I'd learned."

"You hate dragons," Stacy countered. "Why the hell would you bring another one here?"

Damien's eyes brimmed with hatred. "I thought if you were all here, you'd kill one another."

In a way, his plan was working.

"I knew Alerion couldn't survive here for long. Bringing him here would weaken him."

Stacy stilled. "Go on."

Damien stalled, but Diana advanced her blade. "I learned during my research, both through my mother's writings and by investigating other magicals, that creatures from other worlds who have dark magic within them cannot live in this world for long periods without feeding off the magic of that land. Alerion has dark magic, as I've said, so he cannot consume the magic of this world without first contaminating it.

"As you've probably guessed, that is a long, tedious process. He would need hordes of fae here to sustain him and a place for them to come to. That's why he wants to get rid of you and any other dragons first."

Stacy wasn't sure how many other dragons there were. Her

father was perhaps the oldest, but it was possible that there were others. She didn't tell Damien.

Damien sighed. "The more Alerion delves into his dark magic, the weaker he becomes in this world since the magic here is so different from that of Malabbra."

It occurred to Stacy that Alerion was like her, but he represented the other side of the coin. She'd been born of the union of a dragon and a witch, but the good magic of her mother and the long nobility of her father had prevailed. Khan was not driven by Malabbra's influence because he'd never been there. Generations of his kind had existed in the human world. Alerion, on the other hand, had lived there, and the darkness in him had won out despite his father's fae blood.

The pieces fell into place. If she could provoke Alerion into shifting into dragon form, thereby pulling more of his dark magic to the surface, he would be weaker. Then they'd kill him.

Stacy searched Damien's face. "Thank you for the insight. That helps. As for your mother's books, what did you do with them?" Such information and dark magic left sitting around could be dangerous in the wrong hands.

"I destroyed them. I did not want that dark magic to contaminate my home."

If not for Damien's twisted view of magicals, Stacy would have admired his actions. He seemed disgusted by dark magic, as she was, yet he couldn't get past the notion that all magicals were evil. She pitied him. "We could have worked together, but you seemed determined to hate me."

Damien opened his mouth to respond but couldn't find the words.

Stacy nodded at Diana. "Take him inside."

CHAPTER TWENTY-THREE

"Did you ever suspect it?" Stacy had asked Kiera after Damien was taken away.

Kiera's heart thumped wildly. *I knew he had secrets,* she'd thought. He had done horrible things to keep others from learning them, but she had never guessed they were this bad. She'd told Stacy as much.

Kiera scanned the sky as Alerion's roar filled the air. The fight on the ground continued, and if she closed her eyes, she could picture herself on a battlefield on her homeworld, hearing the same clash of weapons, in one or another of the endless civil wars. Other battles had been won before she was born. The fae had subdued the other races on that world, including the sidhe from which her mother had sprung. Here, it wasn't only fae weapons engaging, but the axes and arrows and magic and blades of her friends.

She remembered fighting her way into her father's golden palace with the other assassins from the guild and vowed not to fail this time. This wasn't like how it had been there, with those she'd fought beside willing to sell her out if it let them escape. She loved Stacy, Miles, and Rowan, and she'd come to care for

Ethan, Amy, and the others. She would not let her new family die, and this family would not betray her, no matter what happened.

Kiera summoned her magic, knowing she'd done the first step well. Alerion had been provoked into taking dragon form, and his magic would take a toll on him.

Kiera strode through the forest, kissed by frosty air, shadows folding around her. She did not give in to them yet. Let her father see her coming. She thought about her mother and the other long-dead sidhe and lesser fae and all those on her homeworld who had suffered under his rule. She wouldn't let him do that here.

Kiera stepped out of the trees. The battle zone blazed with magic: fae, elves, wolves, and witches clashing, Rowan and Miles among them. She should be fighting at their sides as they had so many times. Rowan and Miles had not been with her on the fae world, though. They had not faced her father before.

Kiera glanced at the dragon. Her father's scales glowed gold as he spread his wings and rose, displaying his glorious form. He was on the ground, watching as someone approached. Alerion didn't seem to notice that his daughter was nearby. His attention was fixed on Stacy, who strode down the hill, shoulders back and head high. She carried no weapons.

She watched as the human witch strode forth to slay a dragon, and pride filled Kiera. She would die for Stacy.

Stacy dispelled her fear as she marched toward the enormous gold dragon. The closer she got, the more details she noticed. His skin was obsidian, and beneath that swarmed the magic of Malabbra. He seemed to be dipped in gold, but that was a façade conjured by his power.

Stacy's throat was tight and hot, and her heart thumped erratically. Her friends would do all they had to so she would have time to finish this. Finish *him*.

She continued walking forward as Alerion's mouth opened, displaying fangs as white as the moon. His eyes were shaped like hers were in dragon form, but instead of glowing gold like, his matched his flesh. They were so dark that she could not distinguish his serpentine pupils.

Dragons had once roamed this world, and it made sense that they roamed other worlds too. Khan had told her that months ago when he'd shared with her the truth of her heritage. It was as though his voice filled her mind, and she remembered what he'd told her.

Seven dragons were named for the seven elements that built the world. While some preserved life, others sent plagues and destroyed. The cataclysmic events of the Seven Wars drove the dragons away. Some are in hiding, and others fled, never to return.

She was not full of darkness, Stacy reminded herself. She was from a long line of power and strength, but it did not corrupt her.

She halted in front of Alerion. He was much larger than her in her human skin, and he would be in dragon form as well. The dragon's chest heaved with the bloodthirst he contained. He was too curious about her to strike yet, though. A smile curved her lips, then Stacy released a slow, deep breath and muttered, "Here goes nothing."

She shifted.

Stacy had practiced enough that it now happened as naturally as pulling on a coat. Her wings sprouted and spread. Her arms turned to legs and her tail appeared, long and snapping like a whip. Red scales sailed across her body as her human form vanished.

Alerion's voice slammed into her mind. *You are a baby, hardly more than one that has just broken through its egg. You are foolish to fight me when you are so weak. I have walked worlds in this form. I expected more, Drakethorn. You will die easily, crushed to powder.*

When Stacy threw back her head and roared, flames raced up her throat and spewed out. Alerion heaved himself off the ground, narrowly avoiding her fire. Stacy joined him, the ground shaking as she left it. No sooner had she lifted off than he plunged at her, and together, they crashed to the ground.

They twisted and thrashed, a battle of wings and claws and teeth and fire. Alerion could not spew flames, a sure sign that it was taking nearly all his strength to hold onto this form.

Stacy spewed fire again, and he took to the air once more. She flew after him, but he deftly evaded her. How and where he had taken dragon form, she did not know, for he had concealed that ability on his homeworld.

Alerion must have read her thoughts since he rumbled, *I learned long ago how to slip into other worlds unseen and take this form in the wild places where I was free to hunt and fly without being noticed.*

You have come here before! Stacy blurted.

He banked toward her and crashed into her side. She righted herself, but she tore through the tops of several trees. She twisted, and they collided again. Stacy's rage welled, and she engulfed him in another stream of fire, beating him back with wings and claws and teeth.

For a moment, she thought she had weakened him enough to make him land, but he dealt her a mighty blow. His claws caught the edge of one wing and wrenched her toward him. She cried out, the sound unlike that she would have made as a human.

She was upside-down, and he was coming at her. She tried to tear free but couldn't. He struck hard and fast with a clawed foot, and blood poured out of her belly. Pain sheared through her body and plunged cold fingers into her mind. Dark magic clung to the air, and it took all her focus not to lose her grasp on the warm magic within her. Stacy's mind turned hazy, but she had to fight back.

When she slammed into the earth, snow and dirt and debris flew. As he descended toward her, Stacy struggled to turn, but before she could, he landed hard enough to make the ground shake, tail sweeping behind him like a whip. She expected him to strike one last time with claws or teeth.

Instead, Alerion staggered and fell a heap of scales and wings not far from her, too weak to continue. *Get up and finish this*, Stacy commanded herself, but the haze of dark magic that had penetrated her when he wrenched her open prevailed. The last she saw was the night sky, speckled with stars.

Rowan saw them fighting in the air, a flurry of wings and rage. His claws snagged her wing, and he raked her belly open. He cried out as she plummeted toward the ground. If the fall did not kill her…

Rowan didn't let himself finish the thought. Alerion landed close to her with enough force that the ground shook where Rowan stood. Fae warriors lay in heaps around him, their blood soaking the ground and their armor in pieces. The wolves and elves were still fighting, and Ethan and the other witches were elsewhere. Ax dripping fae blood, he took off toward Stacy, heart thundering.

Rowan could hardly hear his boots hitting against the ground or the shrill song of the wind. People were shouting, but he did not pay any attention. The defenders' battle tactics had kept magic moving through the earth, thus weakening Alerion's dark power.

As Rowan hurtled toward the dragons, he saw a pile of gray fur with a bloody neck and. froze. A werewolf lay dead, torn open. His heart skipped a beat, but Rowan carried on. He had been foolish to think they'd lose no one, and he refused to lose *her*.

Rowan reached the crest of the hill behind the mansion and descended. Stacy was not far from him now, still lying on the ground. The end of one wing was torn, and blood still flowed from her wound. She lay on her side, head touching her chest, but she was still breathing.

When he heard a gasp, he spun. Ethan and the witches had followed him. Ethan's face was stricken with panic, eyes fixed on Stacy.

Someone materialized from the shadows by Stacy's side. Kiera bent over her, crying out her name.

Finally, Rowan reached Stacy, chest heaving. Her blood soaked the ground. He glared at Alerion, prepared to hurl his ax at the monster if he attacked, but the king just lay there. He was quickly losing strength, shedding scales one by one despite trying to maintain his dragon form.

Rowan sank to his knees when Kiera yelled, *"We're losing her!"*

It took everything in Ethan not to give into his panic. Seeing Stacy unconscious and bleeding nearly wrenched his heart out of his chest. He dropped down beside Rowan. Kiera was on Stacy's other side.

"We can heal her," a woman called, her voice firm and steady. Ethan twisted to see Elentya running up to them. "We must join our magic, purge the darkness inside her, and close the wound and quickly."

Nox moved forward, as silent as a shadow, magic already at work. Threads of gold wound through her fingers and reached toward the gash in Stacy's belly. No one thought about Alerion or the wounded fae soldiers except Miles, who flung up walls of stone and vines to keep their enemies at bay while they worked.

Ethan had never felt exhaustion so deep, but he pulled on the last threads of his magic, muttering the healing incantation. Nox was next to him, with Demetrius and Diana on his other side. Rowan and Kiera knelt together. Ethan was vaguely aware of Elentya and the Graytails' Alpha standing farther along Stacy's body.

Their magic melded and poured into her wound. Ethan felt the dark magic the fae king had poisoned her with when he struck struggling to take hold. Heart thundering, he yanked the dark threads out.

A moment later, Nox murmured, "It's all out. Now close it."

Stacy would be weak after this was over, perhaps unable to shift back until she recovered, but they could stop the bleeding. Ethan hoped it was not too late. Hot tears filled his eyes, but he forced them back. *Heal, Stacy. Come back to us.*

"Almost there," Nox called.

"We will save her," Elentya assured them.

Ethan let their voices calm him, and finally, Stacy's chest heaved. Her eyes did not open, but she huffed out hot air. Ethan heard a groan and turned. The fae king had lost his dragon form. He lay in the imprint, gasping for air, eyes wild with pain and alarm.

Ethan's breath caught as Kiera rose and drew a dagger from her hip. Her face betrayed nothing as she approached her father and knelt at his side.

Alerion couldn't move. He was too weak.

Kiera surveyed him, wondering if she was caught in a dream where she was about to drive her blade into his heart but would awaken before she could finish the deed. The world was quiet around her. She was unsure if the others were truly struck by silence or if the wind and her tumultuous thoughts were blocking her companions' voices.

Her breathing was erratic after the strain of using her magic on Stacy, but she would have done it again. Would have saved Stacy's life over ending his, even though Stacy wouldn't have wanted that.

Alerion looked different. His face was etched with pain. Stacy hadn't torn him open, but she'd beaten his magic back. Kiera bent over him, and their eyes met.

His rasping voice reached her ears. "Lia...I..."

He couldn't get the rest out. Better that he didn't since nothing he could say would save him. Kiera surveyed the knife she'd drawn, turning the hilt—a simple blade with a silver handle, not the embellished dagger Rowan had given her. "I've never used this before," she whispered. "Only sharpened it. It was my mother's. I took it when I left so she would always be with me, wondering if I would find a noble enough use for it one day. I didn't think I ever would."

Sadness threaded her tone and shone in her eyes. Her voice was thick with emotion as she continued. "I hoped you would change, Father, but you never did, so when Stacy told me your secret and how we could weaken you, I knew it was time."

She continued examining the dagger. She thought about her mother: raped, forced to carry and birth a child, then burned alive. That was enough reason to kill him, even without everything that happened before or since. Even so, Kiera was sorry for what she was about to do.

"For the better of this world and ours," she murmured and met his eyes. "For both worlds. Goodbye, Father." His eyes widened, and he struggled to speak, but no words came, though his face expressed his horror and rage. Kiera Swiftshadow plunged the dagger into his heart.

CHAPTER TWENTY-FOUR

Stacy awoke in a familiar room. Her body ached, and every limb was stiff. When she managed to turn her head enough to see the window, the slightly parted curtains allowed pale morning light to shine through. She realized she was in the bedroom she'd grown up in. She tried to sit up, but every muscle burned with the strain.

She glanced at the worn posters tacked to the walls, the desk and chair covered with dusty books and the trinkets she had not taken with her, and the closet, which contained clothes long out of style. Khan hadn't changed a thing, and Stacy didn't know if she'd ever have the heart to do it herself.

This was the bedroom of a girl who'd not known about her legacy or daunting future. Her only concerns had been completing her homework and getting the holes in her favorite skirt mended.

Finally, Stacy pushed up to her elbows, then to a sitting position. She was alone, and the rest of the house was quiet. The memories from last night rushed back, images flashing through her mind. She recalled hurtling toward the ground, flesh torn and pain almost paralyzing her. She remembered Alerion landing in dragon form and darkness taking her. Voices came to her as well, but she could not place who spoke or what they'd said.

What had happened? Had they won?

Stacy stood, realizing someone had changed her clothes. She must have shifted back to human form while she was unconscious. Khan had warned her that it was possible, but only when her magic was so depleted that her body had no choice. When she stood, she was dizzy and weak.

Stacy wore a comfortable set of pajamas, but her skin and hair were still caked with dirt and blood. She'd take a shower soon. First, she wanted to find everyone else. She padded out of the room to find the upstairs rooms and hall empty. Sunshine poured through the windows as on any other day, and for a moment, it seemed as if last night had been a dream.

Stacy descended to the first floor and heard pans rattling in the kitchen. Esme had come back. The door of her father's library was open, and she slipped it through to find someone dusting the windowsills. "Regi?" she croaked. Gods, she needed water.

He turned, surprise and relief springing into his eyes. "Anastasia, you should be resting."

"Are you *dusting* after all that?"

"I needed to distract myself." He laid the duster down and came toward her, concern knitting his brows. "They told me what happened."

Who was "they," and what the hell had happened? Reginald saw the questions on her face, but he did not explain. He poured a glass of water and handed it to her, and she gulped it down. He tugged her to the nearest sofa, and Stacy realized she was out of breath. "They said you fought Alerion's dragon form well and weakened him enough that when he wounded you, he couldn't do anything else. His dragon form dissolved, and he was left in a vulnerable state."

Reginald's tone was full of pride as he said this, but it turned somber as he continued. "They said you almost died. That without all of them using their magic to purge the dark magic and close the wound, you would have."

Stacy put her hand over his. "Who healed me?"

Reginald's eyes glistened. "All of them. Your friends."

"Alerion?"

"He just laid there. The last thing he witnessed was an act of love and sacrifice—your friends giving all the magic and strength they had left to make sure you didn't leave them."

Stacy's breath caught. "He's dead?"

Reginald nodded gravely. "They told me Kiera did it."

It was right that Kiera had done it. That had been their plan all along, but Stacy's heart ached for her. "Did everyone make it?" she got out at last.

Reginald's expression twisted with sorrow. "Almost everyone. Some of the wolves died, and Elentya lost two of her elves. Demetrius was wounded, but Nox got to him in time. They think he will recover, though it will be a long road."

"You, Amy, and Esme were safe?"

"It was a dreadfully long night of waiting, but no harm came to us."

"Where is everyone?"

"Those who live at your house returned home. Rowan had to haul Ethan out of here." Reginald laughed. "He wanted to remain at your side. Miles was here until dawn taking care of the bodies, and the elves stayed here since we have plenty of room. Nox is tending to them, and Demetrius cannot be moved yet."

"Nox will need to rest."

"You all do, especially *you*."

"What about the Graytails?"

"Went home to bury their kin and mourn."

Tears filled her eyes.

Reginald's face softened. "Do not blame yourself for their

deaths. They fought willingly, knowing that if they had not done so, they would all have died under Alerion's hand."

Stacy nodded, but that didn't make it hurt less. "I should go to them and offer my condolences and…"

Reginald's shaking head made her voice trail off. "Not now. You need to rest."

He was right. Stacy could probably not stand without help, but she was stubborn. "I want to go home and see them. Will you take me there?"

Reginald smiled. "With pleasure." He stood. "Did you enjoy being in your old room? I thought it best you wake up somewhere familiar."

"The whole house is familiar, Regi," Stacy returned with a grin as he helped her up and supported her.

"Yes, but I thought you might like to feel as you once did, without the worries of a dragon legacy."

"And a witch one."

"And a witch one. Without being both, you wouldn't have finished won."

Stacy knew it well.

Stacy wanted to shower before they left, but standing under hot water was a recipe for a blackout, so she took a bath. Esme came in to help and fussed over her for half an hour, tending her cuts and scratches. The process reminded Stacy of days long past when she'd scraped her knee and Esme tended to her with a motherly care she wouldn't have had otherwise. Esme found her suitable clothes to wear home and gave her a long embrace. "Come see us again soon, Stacy. I miss you so much."

Stacy fought off tears. She would come more often, especially now that Torin was gone. She squeezed the old woman's hand. "I promise."

Reginald left her at the front door of her home after letting her know her friends were waiting for her in the library. He had called ahead to inform Rowan and ask that everything be prepared for her return. What "everything" entailed, Stacy did not know, and she was too weary to ask.

When Stacy entered the library, Amy flew over from the window, tears gleaming on her cheeks. "Oh, Stacy!" She flung her arms around her, making Stacy groan at the impact. She winced but embraced Amy.

"I'm so sorry!" Amy backed off, wiping tears from her cheeks. "They told me what happened. That you almost..." Her voice cracked. "It was awful waiting here last night, and this morning when they came back, and you weren't... You..."

Stacy laughed. "I'm okay."

"Let her breathe," Rowan called, followed by a chuckle. Ethan was between Rowan and Miles, with Kiera next to Rowan. Amy told her Diana and Emile were sleeping. Everyone was clearly exhausted, and Stacy wondered if they'd slept.

Miles smiled, and she remembered that he'd spent the rest of the night giving the bodies of the dead fae to the grounds. When Stacy left her father's house, she'd seen no signs of the battle except large imprints of dragons beyond the house. "We're glad to see you, Stacy. It's been a long morning."

Stacy hugged him, then turned to the others. Rowan squeezed her shoulder, and Kiera smiled. Her eyes were haunted, as if she were remembering that she'd killed her father. Stacy would not ask for the full story until Kiera was ready to put words to it.

Ethan pulled her into his arms, whispering into her hair, "I'm so glad to see you."

Stacy had not thought she would cry, but her tears sprang forth. She pulled back, wiping them away. "We did it, didn't we?"

"He's gone," Rowan agreed.

Kiera added, "Forever."

"There's a lot to discuss," Stacy continued.

"You should rest first," Ethan protested.

"I know, but it's on my mind now, and I feel fine, really. I just need to sit." Stacy took the chair by the fireplace, and the others assembled around her. Rowan and Kiera chose the sofa on Stacy's left, and Rowan put his hand on Kiera's knee. Miles leaned against the table, arms folded across his chest. Ethan took the other chair, and Amy plopped onto the sofa opposite Kiera and Rowan.

"I spoke to Agent Davos and Agent Taylor before they took Damien away, and we concluded that there might come a day when everyone knows exactly who I am," Stacy began. "The paranormal community still believes I was responsible for those deaths, though the agents think that when Damien confesses, I'll be in the clear. Regardless, we need to prepare for the attention it will bring. Not all of it will be pleasant."

"We expected that," Amy inserted. "And we're ready. I mean, it can't be worse than what we've already been through, right?"

Murmurs of agreement passed through the room. "Even so," Stacy continued, "our troubles are far from over, but we don't have threat of the fae overtaking our world looming over us. We will work toward a future where we can exist without being killed or considered terrorists and where our races do not misuse our influence to gain power." She thought about Corbinelli and Hines and their allies in the underworld.

"With the increased attention, we should expect life here at the estate to change. We can't just hide here until this passes over, and it's obvious that this is where I live and work." Stacy eyed each of her friends in turn. "Tell me how you feel about that and if you want anything to change."

Kiera cleared her throat. "There is something I want to say."

Everyone turned to her.

"I've been considering it since I first spoke to my father and learned about the sorry state of my homeworld. There is nothing keeping me from going back since his death lifted the banishment curse." Kiera's voice was tinged with raw emotion, a rare moment. "There might still be innocent people there, fighting for their lives against the oppressors my father left behind to rule in his stead—probably my brothers, who are as cruel as he was."

"My homeworld's magic might be nearly depleted, but it can be restored, given time and healing. It's quite possible that the influence of Malabbra lingers in that world, as it does here. I want to see how much of it lurks in the shadows and purge the land if I can."

Kiera's eyes met Stacy's. "I want to go home and see what I can do to help them. That means leaving your service for the time being, but you would do the same thing to help others."

Stacy's heart ached at the thought of Kiera leaving and how empty her home would feel without her, despite Kiera's quiet ways, but she smiled. "You should go, but you must promise we will see one another again."

Kiera shared her smile. "Of course." She motioned around the room. "This has become my home too, and I don't want to leave it forever."

Stacy glanced at Rowan. Conflicting emotions flickered across his face, and his hold on Kiera's knee tightened. Stacy knew what he was worried about. On the one hand, he had long been dedicated to the Thorn estate and its keeping, but after getting Kiera back, he didn't want to leave her side.

His eyes met Stacy's, but she spoke before he could. "Same for you, Rowan. Go with Kiera, but promise we will see one another again."

Tears welled in the dryad's eyes. "I have not left this place since I first came here."

"The house and I will be here when you come back," Stacy assured him. A smile touched her lips. "You are invaluable, Rowan, but we will handle things until you return. Maybe it's time for you to have a new adventure."

"Thank you," Rowan rasped. "I do want to go with her."

Stacy turned to Miles. "Ironwood, what do you think about becoming the new steward of the Thorn estate?"

Miles' eyes had filled when he heard that Rowan and Kiera were leaving. Now, surprise leapt onto his face. "*Me?*"

"I wouldn't trust the place to anyone else. You have a deep connection with the land and are tied to the magic. I want you to take over."

Miles smiled. "I would be honored, Stacy."

Rowan stood, tugging Kiera to her feet beside him. "I would like to speak to Miles and Kiera in the kitchen for a moment." He eyed Stacy. "If you don't mind."

She nodded. "Go ahead." Ethan and Amy remained. Stacy released a long breath. "Now it's us three. I started this journey with the two of you, and I wouldn't have wanted it any other way. I don't think I would have gotten here if we had not become friends."

Amy wiped away a tear. "I'm so glad I took that job to investigate Lenny Dolos and the badass young attorney who wiped the courtroom floor with his ass every other week."

Stacy laughed.

"I'm glad a young, inexperienced witch stumbled upon my shop one day," Ethan inserted.

Stacy stood and opened her arms. Ethan and Amy hugged her, laughter bubbling from their throats. Stacy finally smiled. "Thanks for sticking by me when you found out I was a dragon."

She pulled back as the phone in her back pocket rang. She pulled it out, not knowing who the call could be from, and a smile bloomed on her face.

"Who is it?" Amy asked.

"It's my dad."

EPILOGUE

The grounds were blanketed in tall drifts of snow. A chill wind blew through the trees, and the night sky was clear and speckled with stars. Inside Thorn Manor, fires burned in hearths, and flames danced on candle wicks. The Christmas tree in the living room bore an obscene amount of tinsel, ornaments, and lights, thanks to Amy's and Miles' ministrations.

Rowan was the one who'd called it obscene.

Amy had pinched his cheek. "You're leaving anyway."

The dining room was more beautiful than Stacy had ever seen it. The table was decked with their finest linen and dishes, and the best of Kiera's and Esme's cooking was arrayed across it. "You did a great job with the dining room," she told Rowan and Miles when she entered the kitchen. "Esme and Kiera, everything smells marvelous." The two women bustled between the counters and the stove, putting on the final touches on their Christmas Eve dinner.

Rowan glowered. "Miles could barely get the table set without breaking the heirloom dishes. I don't know how he's going to manage this house."

Miles grinned despite the critique. "Good thing managing the house means I can delegate setting the table to someone else. Isn't the point of being different people that we will do things differently?"

Rowan frowned and switched subjects. "Aren't you going to change into something nicer?"

Miles glanced at his clean overalls and long-sleeve button-down shirt. "This *is* nice!"

"Something more festive, perhaps?" Rowan prodded, the glow in his eyes saying he was pulling the groundskeeper's leg.

Miles' eyes gleamed with amusement. "Fine. I'll find something *festive*." He sauntered out of the kitchen, winking at Stacy. She smiled, shaking her head.

"I don't want to know what he'll produce," Rowan glowered as he reached for two glasses of champagne and handed one to Stacy.

"You should get out of here too," Kiera told Rowan. "We need all the space we can get. Give Esme and me twenty minutes, and dinner will be ready."

Rowan opened his mouth to reply, but Stacy looped her arm through his and led him from the room. "I will worry about this place after I'm gone," he mumbled. Seeing a stray piece of tinsel on the floor, he glared and picked it up.

Rowan had been in a sour mood since this morning because he was suppressing his discomfort about his impending departure. He hadn't changed his mind about going to the fae world with Kiera, but it didn't make leaving the Thorn estate easier. Stacy kept reminding him that they could return whenever they wished. She knew the place would not be the same with Rowan and Kiera and harbored a secret hope that they would not stay in the fae world for long.

Stacy patted his arm. "You will have different things to worry about after you and Kiera leave." She'd persuaded them to stay through Christmas, and they had agreed since Rowan wanted time to transfer the day-to-day management to Miles. Stacy had been searching high and low for a replacement for Kiera. She admitted to Rowan that it was one of the most difficult tasks she'd had since the ordeal with Damien and the fae king, whose name everyone had chosen not to mention after it was over.

"Do you have any prospects?" Rowan asked as they ambled down a hall decorated with garlands and gold ribbons—Amy's doing.

"A few. Interviews start in January," Stacy replied. "For now, I want to enjoy Christmas and pretend nothing will change."

Rowan smiled. "Your mother had the best Christmas Eve parties. Ours might match hers." The party had been Rowan's idea, but Amy, Kiera, and Stacy had planned it.

Stacy checked her watch. "Everyone else should be here soon." She stopped near the front door to check herself in the mirror. Her auburn hair down fell in soft waves to her shoulders, caressing the thick wool of her evergreen sweater. Stacy smoothed her black skirt, admiring the black tights and boots Kiera had given her as an early Christmas present.

Footsteps behind them caused Stacy and Rowan to turn to see Amy gliding down the stairs wearing a short cherry-red dress and black tights like Stacy's. Her golden hair glowed in the candlelight, making her look angelic. "Well?" she asked, twirling for them when she reached the bottom.

"Delightful," Rowan answered.

"Gorgeous, as always." Stacy kissed her cheek.

Amy stopped spinning and smiled. "Good, because I was hoping another guest would like it and you wouldn't be mad at me for inviting someone else."

Rowan arched a brow. "Who might that be?"

"A date," Amy replied sheepishly. "The werewolf named Elliot from Khan's Pennsylvania estate."

Stacy, who was sipping champagne while Amy said this, nearly choked. After managing to swallow, she burst out, "Since when have you been talking to Elliot?"

Amy shrugged. "I found him online and sent a friend request. We've been chatting ever since."

A chuckle alerted the trio to Ethan's presence as he ambled in from the living room, hands deep in his dress slacks' pockets. Like Stacy, he wore a wool sweater, but his was navy. He put an arm around Stacy while grinning at Amy. "Amy's invited a date to our Christmas Eve party?"

"What? He's cute!"

Stacy and Ethan shared a laugh. Rowan shook his head.

Amy glowered and pointed at the couple. "Once upon a time, you two pretended you weren't obsessed with each other!"

Whatever might have followed was interrupted by a booming voice on the staircase and Miles' heavy steps descending. *"HO HO HO!"*

Rowan buried his face in his hands.

"Oh. My. Fucking..." Amy started.

Ethan burst out laughing. Stacy gaped.

Miles arrived on the first floor clad in a Santa Clause costume, beard and all. "Rowan told me to find something more festive, and it doesn't get any more festive than this."

"Where the hell did you find that?" Rowan demanded.

Miles' brown eyes sparkled. "I've always had it."

There was a knock on the front door, and Rowan went to open it. On the porch, arms piled high with presents, stood Khan and Reginald, wearing long black coats and smiles. Their smiles faltered when they saw Miles in the bright red get up. When the two men moved closer to the door, Stacy noticed someone behind them.

Elliot stepped into the hall behind the older men, his cheeks red from the cold. Amy beamed and went to greet him.

Rowan took their gifts and transported them to the living room. The others moved aside to allow Khan and Reginald into the hallway while Amy whisked Elliot off to show him the house. Smiling, Khan kissed his daughter's cheek. "I don't know why the groundskeeper of one of my other estates is here. I take it you have a good reason?"

Stacy merely smiled.

"Thank you for inviting us," he added. "This reminds me of the parties your mother used to throw."

Stacy thought about how matters had evolved over the past few weeks. When Khan had called, he'd apologized for not being in touch, explaining that he had been "putting the vampires in their place." It hadn't been a pretty business, he'd added, and he'd promised to tell her about it when he saw her. Khan had promised to return for Christmas and had arrived home a few days ago.

That first night back, Stacy had gone to the house for dinner, and father and daughter had shared a long conversation in his library before the fire afterward. Reginald had told Khan that he'd informed Stacy of the true circumstances surrounding her mother's death. "I'm sorry I kept it from you all these years," Khan had said, deep sorrow on his face.

Before he could say more, Stacy had laid a hand on his. "I understand. I'm just glad I know now."

She'd told him about the ordeal with the fae and Damien and her ongoing difficulties with those left prowling the underworld and the paranormal community who were skeptical of her intentions. It would all work out as it was supposed to, she had assured him, and life was otherwise back to normal.

"Or as normal as life can be for a dragon," she'd added, smiling with hints of gold gleaming in her eyes. Khan wrapped an arm around her, and as she led him toward the dining room, she hoped the next week would be a time of rest and enjoyment.

Miles, Amy, and Ethan filed in behind them, chatting. Rowan came in last, stating that the Graytails and Elentya had sent gifts as well, and they could open them later. Kiera and Esme bustled in a moment later, bringing the last dishes.

Stacy took her place at the head of the table and smiled at her guests. She could not imagine her life being more perfect than it was at that moment. She raised her glass of champagne. "Thank you, everyone, for joining me here tonight. I can't imagine a better group of people to spend my evening with. Merry Christmas!"

Everyone else raised their glasses, echoing her toast.

Stacy sat, mouth watering. "Now, let's eat. I'm starving."

Afterward, Stacy slipped through the back door and wandered toward the Guardian's Grove, desiring a moment of quiet despite the chill air. She tramped through the snow, heedless of it getting into her boots and soaking her stockings. The trees glistened with ice, and though the temperature turned Stacy's cheeks pink, a smile graced her lips. She placed her hand over her mother's locket, grateful for its steadying warmth. "I feel you here tonight, Mom. This was for you as much as it was for them."

She glanced at the house over her shoulder, warm at the thought of her friends inside, laughing and talking. Stacy imagined how pale her life would have turned out in comparison if she hadn't come to this house or met those people.

She finally came to a halt amid the Guardian trees. Sprites flitted about, gold orbs dancing among the branches. Stacy did not hear footsteps, but she sensed her father behind her. She turned, wearing a soft smile.

Khan did not speak as he came to her side, surveying the area thoughtfully. Their long, companionable silence was comfortable, and Stacy wanted it to last much longer. Finally, Khan broke the silence. "I'm very proud of you."

Stacy turned, surprised to see tears glistening in his eyes.

He cleared his throat. "You have everything in hand, but I will be around when you want or need me."

"But?" she prodded.

He smiled. "It has been a long time since I have done any casual traveling. Not since your mother and I took our honeymoon, actually."

Stacy chuckled. "Where do you plan to go?"

Khan gave their surroundings an appraising look. "Somewhere warm. Funny, I don't yet own a beach house."

Stacy rolled her eyes. "About that. We need to discuss your property. You don't need it all."

"Do whatever you wish, but keep this place. I never want to lose the home where Catherine had you and you grew up."

"I will," Stacy agreed, reaching for his hand. She squeezed it, then held it, and the comfortable silence returned. She had not imagined that bringing him a lasagna months ago would have turned into all this. As she looked at her father, she realized all she had ever wanted was to make him proud.

I don't need to feel that way anymore. Stacy leaned her head on his shoulder. "Thank you for coming tonight. Everyone was happy to have a party."

Khan's eyes glistened again. "I am so pleased that you have found a family, Stacy, beyond you and me."

She smiled. "I am, too. I think Mom would be proud of how far we have come."

Khan did not wipe away the tear that rolled down his cheek. He smiled, his eyes meeting hers. "She would."

AUTHOR'S NOTES

OCTOBER 22, 2024

Thank you for reading the (current) final book in this series! It was a fun ride for me. I hope you enjoyed it as well.

I am now writing an urban fantasy series called Claudia Richelieu: The Chimera Agent, and it's the Spiderking Universe, full of vampires and other supernatural beings. The first book is Shadows of Prejudice, and it published on 15 October. You can order it at Shadows of Prejudice I am hard at work on book 3 now. Book two will publish on 12 November, and you can preorder it here Burn With Prejudice

The first book in the wide Spiderking universe is Secret Inheritance

That series is my first endeavor in this new world, and if that goes well, I will write a bounty hunter series in the same universe. Aside from that...

Scandals in Conkerland

As the New York Times put it:

It could have come straight from the plot of a Shakespearean tragedy.

AUTHOR'S NOTES

A king is challenged to a battle by a young pretender, with victory earned only by the destruction of the other. The king emerges triumphant, but there is suspicion that he has acted nefariously in the tussle for the crown.

Conkers is a uniquely UK sport, although I followed this scandal, there being little else to do in the rainy autumn besides take Emma for walks and bake too much. I mean, the cheese rolling and welly wanging competitions were over for the year, so what else was I to do?

What are conkers, you ask? We didn't indulge in this, but our Nat told me that in her schoolyard, children picked up the seeds of the chestnut tree, or conkers, somehow tied a string around them, and whaled the daylights out of their friends with them. I managed to avoid this delight during my formative years. Obviously, no chestnut trees grew in my schoolyard or neighborhood, or the boys would have perpetrated that outrage.

Skip lightly through the years to adulthood, and you get the World Conkers Championship held yearly in Northamptonshire, England. This year, Southwick was the site of the competition. The combatants...I mean, participants beat each others' conkers to a pulp, not their skulls. I am sure they miss, but it is an improvement.

This year, the crowned king was accused of cheating by using a metal nut! Can you imagine? Horrors!

Cliffhanger...I shall report the final results in my next author notes!

The usual business

I always have to thank LMBPN's staff for making my journey to publication as painless as they could. From the beta team who suggests improvements to the series to Kelly O, who does everything, to the editor who smooths my prose to the just-in-time team who catches last-minute errors, it is a joy working with you!

Thank you for taking a chance on my series! If you enjoy it and you have a moment, leaving a review would be very helpful for me (as it is for any writer).

I look forward to catching up with you in the next book.

Izzie Campbell

BOOKS FROM ISABEL

The Chronicles of the WitchBorn
(with Michael Anderle)
The First Witch-Mage (Book 1)
The Witch-Mage Awakens (Book 2)
The Witch-Mage Liberation (Book 3)
The Witch-Mage Uprising (Book 4)
The Witch-Mage Breaking (Book 5)
The Witch-Mage Ascending (Book 6)
Witch-Mage Convergence (Book 7)
Witch-mage Legacy (Book 8)

The Magic Academy of Paris
(with Michael Anderle)
The Forbidden Incantations (Book 1)
The Treacherous Alchemy (Book 2)
The Cursed Enchantments (Book 3)
The Perilous Secrets (Book 4)
The Sinister Onslaught (Book 5)
A Resilient Requiem (Book 6)

BOOKS FROM ISABEL

Drakethorn Legal
(With Michael Anderle)
A Witch's Legacy (Book 1)
Scales of Truth (Book 2)
The Drake Defense (Book 3)
The Mantle Returns (Book 4)
Legal Flames (Book 5)
When Justice Has Claws (Book 6)

Claudia Richelieu: The Chimera Agent
(With Michael Anderle)
Shadows of Prejudice (Book 1)
Burn With Prejudice (Book 2)

CONNECT WITH THE AUTHORS

Connect with Isabel Campbell

Facebook: https://www.facebook.com/IsabelCampbell.author

Website: http://isabelcampbellauthor.com/

Connect with Michael Anderle

Website: http://lmbpn.com

Email List: https://michael.beehiiv.com/

https://www.facebook.com/LMBPNPublishing

https://twitter.com/MichaelAnderle

https://www.instagram.com/lmbpn_publishing/

https://www.bookbub.com/authors/michael-anderle

OTHER LMBPN PUBLISHING BOOKS

To be notified of new releases and special promotions from LMBPN publishing, please join our email list:

http://lmbpn.com/email/

For a complete list of books published by LMBPN please visit the following pages:

https://lmbpn.com/books-by-lmbpn-publishing/

BOOKS BY MICHAEL ANDERLE

Sign up for the LMBPN email list to be notified of new releases and special deals!

https://lmbpn.com/email/

For a complete list of books by Michael Anderle, please visit:

www.lmbpn.com/ma-books/

www.ingramcontent.com/pod-product-compliance
Lightning Source LLC
LaVergne TN
LVHW041921070526
838199LV00051BA/2695